CHEERS FOR L.B. GREENWOOD!

"Written with the blessings of the Conan Doyle estate and with good reason...SHE PRESERVES THE LATE AUTHOR'S ACHIEVEMENT: the complicated and readable interplay between the precise, brilliant Holmes and the perpetually baffled, yet utterly lovable Watson." —*Booklist*

"RATES HIGH MARKS for adherence to the Holmes canon as well as for a MYSTERY THAT CAN STAND ON ITS OWN MERITS." —*John Barkham Reviews*

"HAIL THE RETURN OF FICTION'S BEST LOVED DETECTIVE. Holmes' fans will delight in this latest adventure...a marvelously intricate mystery in its own right that will also satisfy Holmes devotees who long for just one more adventure. Greenwood has captured the wonderfully acerbic character of Holmes." —*Rave Reviews*

"Bright, brisk...As much gothic as mystery, but without the silliness and stuffiness that afflict most attempts to concoct newly discovered, never published manuscripts from the hand of Dr. Watson." —*Kirkus Reviews*

"It is exactly the sort of faithful, straightforward, entertaining Sherlock Holmes mystery that we like to see." —Jon L. Lellenberg, BSI (the Conan Doyle estate)

"Pure Holmes and Watson, as we know and love them, with no rude intruders from outside the Holmesian universe to cloud our enjoyment." —Elizabeth Peters, author of *Lion in the Valley*

Sherlock Holmes

and the Case of the
Raleigh Legacy

L. B. Greenwood

ST. MARTIN'S PRESS / NEW YORK

Grateful acknowledgment to Dame Jean Conan Doyle for permission to use the Sherlock Holmes characters.

SHERLOCK HOLMES AND THE CASE OF THE RALEIGH LEGACY

Copyright © 1986 by L. B. Greenwood

All rights reserved.

Published by arrangement with Atheneum

Library of Congress Catalog Card Number: 86-47678

ISBN: 0-312-90843-1   Can. ISBN: 0-312-90845-8

Printed in the United States of America

First St. Martin's Press mass market edition/November 1987

10 9 8 7 6 5 4 3 2 1

FOR V.K.

Always remembered, always loved.

MIDNIGHT, and I sit alone before a dying fire in our Baker Street rooms. If I pull the curtains aside, I know that I will see the yellow globes of streetlights casting their wavering and sulphureous circles on the deserted pavement, with all between dark and hidden. The sound of Big Ben drifts fitfully to me, its notes dispersed and scattered by the wind so that it is a ghost clock that intones the hour of the dead. Holmes is out on the track of a new case and will not be home tonight, my old wound aches, and I shiver.

I close my eyes, and at once from the distant past of this land, dim and silent, those four figures glide into my blank sight: Queen Elizabeth, wigged and jewelled, imperious and passionate; Bess Throckmorton, her maid of honour, high bosom bare above the tight lacing, almond eyes at once shrewd and sensuous; Sir Walter Raleigh, pirate, courtier extraordinaire, with dark gaze hot for love or war; and in the corner, fingering his food-stained beard with dirty fingers, the bent and troubled figure of James the First.

I rouse with a start and stare at the calendar: midnight has come and gone, it is now October 29, and there will be no sleep for me tonight.

Then so be it! Let them come, let them guide my pen. Though this account cannot be published during my lifetime, I will set down the tangled events that led to Holmes' stunning revelation of the secret legacy of Sir Walter Raleigh and of the great treasure of his wife, Bess Throckmorton.

"The knowledge of the wicked is ignorance"

Sir Edward Coke, prosecutor at the treason trial of
Sir Walter Raleigh

HOLMES' part in the Raleigh case began some
months after he and I began sharing lodgings. I, in-
valided home from medical service in India, was still in
the midst of the tiring search for a practice which would
not be beyond both my health and pocketbook. As I
wearily entered our rooms at 221B Baker Street on a
sultry August day, I was struck by the rare opportunity
to turn the tables on my fellow lodger, who often seemed
to take perverse delight in teasing me with his deductions.

So, while hanging up my hat, I casually observed that
Holmes had recently had a visitor.

Those deceptively hooded grey eyes, with an amused
glint lurking within, turned upon me. "Is Saul also
among the prophets? By what evidence do you arrive
at your conclusion, doctor?"

"By the irrefutable evidence," I replied more than a
little triumphantly, "of the papers, which were occupy-
ing your attention when I left, now lying in a corner
of the bookcase; of a room which is as hot as an oven
and as thick with smoke as a November morn with fog;

and, moreover, of Mrs. Hudson's urgent request, as I passed through the downstairs hallway, to know if you were not ready for supper as you had had nothing since breakfast. She added that you had been 'eating like an angel' all the time I have been away; hence my presumption that a new case has only recently come to your attention."

With a chuckle Sherlock Holmes knocked out the last dottle from his pipe. "Your evidence is hardly irrefutable, doctor. You could, I think, safely assume that my interest in English country dialects (the subject of those papers now in the bookcase) has waned before the arrival of a more interesting problem, but it could have come to my attention by way of the mail, a telegram, a messenger—even the newspapers. Your assumption that I have had a visitor is thus going beyond the facts at your disposal."

"Then I am wrong?" I dropped with a tired sigh into my chair.

"As it happens, you are quite right—which in itself provides a salutary lesson to those interested in the deductive method. Was your journey to Marley successful, by the way?"

"I hardly know," I replied, more than a little sourly, for I had just returned from that small seasonal resort where I had been looking at a practice which had been advertised in *The Lancet*. "The price asked is commensurate with the length of the patient list, and yet . . ."

"You are not inclined to make the purchase?"

"I suppose that I am not yet far enough from the

sick bed myself to face with equanimity the care of a steady succession of invalids," I replied. "Now that you ask me, Holmes, I find that I can say that I definitely will not buy that practice."

"I am glad that you are apt to remain a gentleman of leisure for some time yet, for my recent visitor has presented me with a problem in which your help could well prove invaluable."

"Then my time is certainly at your disposal."

"Capital," Holmes replied with a satisfaction which did much to revive my flagging spirits. "Open the window, doctor, while I ring for the supper which our good landlady is so anxious to serve us. Then I shall tell you all, and you, if you will be so good, will in turn enlighten me."

As it happened, we were both hungry enough to launch our combined onslaught on the cold joint in silence, and so it was not until we were back in our easy chairs, glasses in hand, that Holmes resumed his narration. He did so by taking up from the table by the visitor's chair a small notepad and passing it over to me.

"Can you guess what gentleman of your acquaintance made this idle sketch while engaged in conversation with me?"

The drawing was of the corner of a shingled roof with under it a sash window, obviously executed quickly, yet done with some skill and apparent accuracy.

"I can think of no one," I soon replied. "Of course I seem to know so few people now."

"Yet Mr. Moseley—"

"Mr. Moseley!"

"None other than Mr. Ivor Moseley of Nightstead. I received a note from him yesterday, asking to see me to discuss a problem of an unstated nature. He had, he stated, heard of me through a recent letter which appeared in *The Times*."

"I wish that I had seen it. No doubt it appeared while I was away?"

"It did, yes. A certain elderly clergyman wrote to the editor to express his satisfaction with the way that a Mr. Sherlock Holmes of Baker Street had quickly and discreetly solved a personal problem which had caused the good vicar much acute distress."

"I do not remember a clergyman among your more recent callers," I remarked. "If he had been a rat catcher, or possibly one of several assorted dustmen—"

"You have not yet become accustomed to my unorthodox visitors," Holmes replied, his eyes twinkling. "Though as a matter of fact, I do not think that you were at home when the clergyman called, and his problem was so simple that I was back here myself by late afternoon. He believed that his daughter had been murdered."

"The problems which you call simple, Holmes!"

"Certainly, when the pool of spilled blood is nothing more than dye with which the daughter had attempted to disguise the grey hairs which she feared would constitute a barrier between herself and the newly expected curate."

"You traced the lady?" As always, I was amused by

Holmes' detached way of reducing the seemingly bizarre to the completely ordinary.

"There was no great difficulty. Being a novice at the art of hair colouring, the daughter had produced such a startling transformation that she had precipitously fled to the house of an old servant, in her agitation dropping the note which was to explain her sudden disappearance. The dye was of a slightly sticky nature, and the note, adhering to the lady's shoe, left a mark in the soft earth of the shrubbery which was quite unmistakable.

"As for your friend Mr. Moseley, when he called this morning he began by saying that, though he did not know if a family secret lay within my field of investigation, he was quite desperate and would appreciate any advice that I could offer. And I nearly did refuse him, for puzzles of the past centuries are hardly in my line."

"Then Mr. Moseley's family secret *is* the Raleigh legacy," I asked eagerly, "and you *are* going to accept the case?"

Holmes gave me a keen glance over his glass. "So you do know something of the matter. As I hoped, for whether or not Mr. Moseley's family secret becomes my case seems at the moment to depend upon what you can tell me."

"But—"

"I am as yet nearly totally lacking in the background information which will almost certainly prove vital, for Mr. Moseley really had very little to say—indeed, he left rather abruptly after giving me a paper which he said was the crux of the whole matter. (He seriously overrates its importance, I fear.) That little notebook which I showed you happened to be lying on the table by Mr. Moseley's chair, and as he talked he picked up a pencil and made a few rapid lines on the paper; that sketch is the result. Could you produce such a drawing, Watson?"

I shook my head. "Beyond what lies in the field of medical anatomy, I am useless with a pencil."

"And I am little better: certainly my fingers would never compose such a drawing during a brief conversation." Holmes tossed the notebook in a drawer of his desk and, rather to my surprise, locked it. "Now doctor, what can you tell me about Mr. Moseley and his family mystery? What is the connection with Sir Walter Raleigh?"

As I was gathering my thoughts, I suddenly remembered a sheaf of papers which I had come across only a few days before, and, hastening off to my room, returned with a large and well-filled envelope.

"Holmes," I said, presenting my offering with a flourish, "you have here all I know of Mr. Ivor Moseley, his stepson Alexander Raleigh, their strange abode of Nightsead, and the legacy of Sir Walter Raleigh."

"And how, pray, did it happen that you had their story so conveniently ready for me?" Holmes was rapidly pulling out the three dozen or so pages which the envelope contained.

"The simplest answer," I replied, "and the truest is: boredom. Before I came to share lodgings with you, I was staying at the Strand. One day I was sitting in the lounge, as listless as a dog in summer, when a periodical at which I was idly glancing fell open to an announcement of a contest for the writing of a short romance."

"Watson, do you mean that these pages—"

"Wait," I held up a cautionary hand. "I knew well enough that I was totally incapable of composing even a brief piece of romantic fiction, but while I had been a student at the University of London, I had been an observer of a sequence of events in the life of a friend which I had long thought held all the qualities of a good yarn."

"So you ordered up a ream of paper, a bottle of ink, a dozen pens, and set to work," Holmes replied, tossing the pages onto the table. "A romance, my dear fellow, is still a romance, and of precious little use to me. I want facts."

"That is precisely what you have there," I replied triumphantly. "I began by making as exact a record of people and occurrences as I could, of course intending later to transform and expand my first jottings in a way which would at once increase interest and protect identity."

"And did you do so?" Holmes had taken up my discarded pages with quickened interest.

I shook my head. "I found that, do what I might, unadorned truth remained just that and my hoped for romance a mere chimera of the mind. These pages of factual account ended up at the bottom of my trunk and were unearthed only the other day, when I was sorting through my old possessions. They tell of events which, in the main, happened some four years ago."

"Then let us hope that your title has more truth than fancy to it," Holmes returned, "for at the moment, while there is something puzzling about Mr. Moseley's approach to me . . . Good night, doctor."

The pages which follow are those I gave Holmes, and they bear the title which I had originally planned for my stillborn romance.

WHEN one attends an institute of higher learning on a very limited income, one must expect to live poorly. During my years in medical studies at the University of London, I resided in a tumbledown lodging-house on a miserable little cul-de-sac off Portland Place. Whatever the weather in more fortunate regions, under that battered old roof the summers were always stifling, the winters immensely frigid, and the air impregnated with the aroma of rancid grease. No matter: I was young, my lodging cheap, my studies fascinating, and life seemingly all before me.

In my second to last year at the university, the single room next to my very modest chambers was taken by Alexander Raleigh, a tall, slender, blond fellow several years younger than I, with a curiously self-contained air and an abrupt, though courteous, manner. All I could then have said of his work was that it seemed to involve Aleck's spending nearly every day at the Reading Room of the British Museum and half every night writing by the light of a lone tallow candle.

Then near the end of my own academic term I was

called away by family matters. (These concerned my unfortunate elder brother, but his unhappy fate has no further place in this account.) I was away for six weeks and returned to face a summer lying dismally fallow before me and a purse seriously depleted. I had hoped to find a temporary position which would both fill my hours and somewhat replenish my pocketbook, but too many others had been before me, and all posts had been taken.

On the day when the last of my inquiries had been negatively answered, I trudged up to my chambers in such deep dejection that I was hardly aware of the solitary figure toiling wearily ahead of me. Only when he stopped at the door next to mine did I recognize Alexander Raleigh.

"Aleck!" I exclaimed, too shocked to think of how slight our acquaintance was. "Whatever has happened to you?" For though he had always been spare of flesh, now his very clothes appeared to hang as from a skeleton, and his light hazel eyes seemed to float bodilessly in the bleached pallor of a young face once ruddy with health.

He shrugged. "I've been off my fodder a bit of late, that's all." In spite of his brave words, he was leaning against the jamb of his door as if it were an effort even to remain upright.

"Have you seen a doctor?" I demanded.

"Oh yes. Here," he led the way into his tiny room and, before collapsing on the bed, tossed me a letter from his book-strewn table.

The letter was addressed to a Mr. Ivor Moseley of Nightsead, stated that Aleck's failing health had no obvious cause, and that should he not soon improve he should seek further medical advice. It was signed by Dr. Abernathy, a retired physician who lived downstairs and was the regular source of help for all on that poor street.

I returned the letter to Aleck. "Mr. Moseley is. . . ?"

"My stepfather. He has been insisting that I return to Nightsead and start reading law at old Roundtree's in the village, and I . . . I won't do it, Jack. I'm going to stay here, somehow, to go on with my work."

"I have never understood what your work is, Aleck."

He grinned wryly. "Neither does my stepfather. The trouble is that I've lived with the music of the Elizabethan poets in my head for so long that I can't now bring myself to jog along to any other tune."

"But if you mean that you wish to become an Elizabethan scholar, surely you should be at Oxford or Cambridge?"

"No money," Aleck replied succinctly. "You see, my father died before I was born, leaving to my mother all that he had, and *she* died when I was very young, leaving everything to my stepfather."

"With no provision for you at all?"

"I was commended to my stepfather's care until I come of age," Aleck answered drily, "which I shall do next week. That's the rub, you see, Jack: legally my stepfather can then toss me out as a bit of spoiled rubbish."

"Surely you're not suggesting——"

"Well, no, he's a decent enough fellow, I suppose, although . . . Anyway, I must admit that he inherited little enough from my mother except the use for life of the very ruinous ruins of my ancestral home. And he did agree to finance a year for me in London, if I kept my expenses down to the minimum. But that year is up, and he says that I've wasted my time and his money, that I must stop doing both. In short, that I must go home and start reading law at Roundtree's."

"Is your home far from London?"

Aleck gave a short, hard laugh. " 'Home' is really the wrong word, unless for ghosts of the very far and unknown past. The place is called Nightsead, and I will not live there, or in the village, for the rest of my life. *I will not*."

I was more than a little startled by the ferocity in Aleck's quiet voice and asked hesitantly, "You really have nothing, nothing at all, of your own?"

"Not a damn penny. Unless," he added with a rueful grin, "you count the Raleigh legacy, left by the great Sir Walter."

"I didn't know that you had such a historic ancestry, Aleck," I exclaimed.

"Well, there are some limbs missing from the family tree, unfortunately, but at least I've written to the lawyers, and they say that, as the son of my father, my claim is good."

"But if you have an inheritance coming to you so soon——"

At that Aleck laughed. The Raleigh legacy, he explained, consisted of a sealed envelope which had forever to remain in the hands of a firm of London lawyers. The contents could be seen by the heir when he came of age and thereafter as often as he wished, but they could never be shown to anyone else, nor ever removed from safekeeping.

"What a curious inheritance!" I wondered. "Whatever do you think is in the envelope?"

"Some scrap of paper which was once very precious to someone and yet is meaningless enough now," Aleck replied. "A letter from the queen to Sir Walter, perhaps."

"Then why all the secrecy?"

Aleck shrugged. "Political reasons of the time, probably; it was a period of really intense intrigues, you know. At any rate, I shall certainly claim my strange legacy, whatever it is, on my birthday next week. Mind that you dine with me that night, Jack, to celebrate."

"I shall do so with pleasure," I replied, "but unless your health improves during the interval, it seems to me that our dinner will consist of a Bath biscuit and a glass of water."

Aleck grinned. "If mine does, I promise that yours will be more splendid."

"It shall indeed," I retorted, "for I will provide it. No, Aleck, I insist: your birthday feast shall be in my rooms."

And on that we finally agreed.

I made a point of seeing Aleck, even if briefly, every

day during the next week, but I was as little pleased with his progress towards health as with my own towards employment. Aleck remained thin and white, though still dragging himself daily to the B.M., and I remained without any prospects of a position for the summer.

On the morning of Aleck's birthday, I called on him to offer my good wishes and found with him his stepfather, newly arrived from the country. He was a tall and slender man of surprisingly youthful appearance, very dark of hair and eye, with prominent cheekbones and a thin face, unexpectedly heavy lips and a narrow chin, softly spoken and neatly dressed in an old-fashioned frock coat.

He had, he explained to me, come to London in order to help Aleck pack for his return to Nightsead. To this Aleck made no answer, but his face was so grim that I, after including Mr. Moseley in my supper invitation, was glad to return to my rooms.

Aleck's mood had not lightened by evening: when Mr. Moseley and I drank his good health, he pointedly returned only my toast, and when I hastily asked, "Now, Aleck, do tell us: what *is* your legacy?", it was obvious from Mr. Moseley's alert expression that he had as yet had no information from Aleck.

"My legacy, Jack, is about what I expected: a single sheet of handmade paper, covered on both sides with faded writing."

"And the subject of the writing?" Mr. Moseley unwisely interjected.

"Is not your concern, sir," Aleck replied, and every word was cold steel. For several moments there was a silence that I, at least, was too embarrassed to break. Then Aleck, nearly turning his back on his stepfather, added, "In any case, Jack, I can hardly tell myself what the letter is about. It seems to be the kind which would make sense only to the writer and his correspondent."

"It is not addressed to anyone?" I asked. "Or signed?"

Aleck hesitated. "Not by name."

"By initials?" I suggested.

Aleck shook his head.

"By a device of some kind?" Mr. Moseley offered. "A common enough Elizabethan practice, after all."

"As you say, sir, it was common," Aleck replied frigidly.

There was another period of silence, which I tried to fill by attending to our glasses. "You don't think that your legacy has any value, then, Aleck?" I ventured.

"I don't see how it can have," he replied, and though his voice was steady and his face calm, I knew that his last small hope of remaining in London had that afternoon died. "From my own work of the past year, I would judge that the paper and handwriting *are* Elizabethan, but since I am forbidden to remove the letter from the lawyer's care, I couldn't sell it even if I wished. No, I can see no commercial value in my precious legacy. Although—" he stopped abruptly.

"Although what?" I demanded eagerly. Strange how

the very idea of treasure arouses our human frailty! But my too great curiosity received the rebuke it deserved: another of Aleck's quick shrugs.

More silence. "At least the letter could be from Sir Walter Raleigh?" I suggested.

But Aleck shook his head. "On the contrary, Jack. Now that I have seen it, I am positive that it is not."

"Or from Queen Elizabeth?"

"No, most definitely not."

"Who knows if the letter is even genuine?" Mr. Moseley added with a sigh.

At once my friend fired, his hazel eyes blazing like powder. "You think the letter spurious, do you, sir?"

"My dear boy, I do not 'think' on the subject at all, for I know nothing about it. I merely observe that the instructions which go with your legacy *are* strange, seemingly designed to prevent an expert examination of the paper, and that, if the letter were the prank of some jesting ancestor of yours, that would explain the whole matter. That is all."

At this point our supper was brought in. Knowing my friend's weakened condition, I had ordered the simplest of meals, but as far as poor Aleck was concerned, I believe it would have made no difference if we had had the hottest of Indian curries, the richest of pastries, and the oldest of ports. For though Aleck ate quite heartily, the meal was hardly over before he suddenly rose and hastily asked to retire to my bed chamber.

And within a few minutes there came the ominous sounds of sickness, together with a crash. Of course Mr.

Moseley and I rushed in, to find Aleck sitting on the side of my bed, the jordan before him, the room reeking of kerosene, and on the floor the broken fragments of a small bedside lamp which in his necessary haste he had knocked flying: bits of the chimney and pieces of the bowl were nearly under Aleck's feet, and the burner had rolled half-way across the room. His attack of illness was violent but fortunately of short duration, and I— he would have no assistance from his stepfather—was soon able to help the poor fellow back to his own room. I urged him to allow me to summon Dr. Abernathy, but Aleck would not hear of it, and as he was by then resting comfortably, I thought it expedient to suggest that Mr. Moseley return to have a final glass of wine in my chambers.

Once there I took the opportunity to press upon him the desirability of leaving Aleck, at least for a few weeks longer, in town.

"If it were only a matter of a little more expense," Mr. Moseley replied quietly, "I would somehow find the money. But the problem, Mr. Watson, lies in Aleck's temperament. He wishes to lead the life of an unpaid scholar: a worthy aim, but impossible for a poor man. Aleck must accordingly prepare himself for a more practical future."

"Reading law in Mr. Roundtree's office in the village," I interjected. "Or so Aleck has told me that you have urged."

"Because I can think of nothing else that is open to him. Nor can he. But being Aleck, he simply must struggle before he submits, poor boy. Mr. Watson, Aleck has told me that you have no fixed plans for the summer. Would you consider spending the time with us at Nightsead?"

I am sure that I gaped with astonishment.

"You have no idea how much good you could do Aleck," Mr. Moseley continued, his dark eyes fixed most seriously on mine, "for it is surely evident by now that his current weakness is nervous in origin. He was never ill during his boyhood years at Nightsead; it is this longing for what is impossible that is destroying him, poor fellow. Join us at Nightsead, Mr. Watson, and help convince my poor lad that he must accept the inevitable."

I at once put the proposition to Aleck; the immediate brightening of his pale face was all the answer that I required.

So I came to spend the summer weeks surrounded by one of the most extraordinary ruins of England.

We began our journey as soon as the sun was well up the sky by taking a cab to Paddington Station, on that hot summer day crowded with holiday makers.

"Where *is* Nightsead?" I asked Mr. Moseley as we waited for our tickets, jostled by surly fathers, impatient mothers and crying children.

"In the outer reaches of the Cotswolds. Do you know the area at all, Mr. Watson?"

I did not, but even I had heard of the beauty of the rolling hills and said as much.

At my side Aleck gave a small and sardonic grin.

"Even the Cotswolds have their geological lapses, Jack. You're in for some surprises."

"Not all unpleasant ones, I hope," Mr. Moseley interposed.

"I can think of none which are not," Aleck retorted, and thereafter we were all largely silent.

What an interminable day that was! We made our first change of trains at Reading, and were forced to cool our heels for over an hour before the connecting train for Swindon arrived; there we waited again for nearly two hours.

"At least," I suggested hopefully, "we must now have covered the greater part of our journey."

"In miles, yes," Aleck replied briefly. "In time, no."

He was all too accurate. We moved from one small stopping point to another, never having more shelter than that of a small station-house invariably furnished with benches peculiarly designed to offend the human form, and with no more refreshment than spongy cheese, stale bread and weak beer purchased at a neighbouring public house.

Nor by then was the scenery such as to lift the spirits. We had begun bravely, moving through a landscape so lovely that I inwardly exclaimed, " 'This other Eden!' " The flat banks of the innumerable streams were high with succulently waving grasses and proudly tossing reeds, the open heath spread its bounty in a myriad of colours, and the frequent villages with their slate or thatched roofs were clean and warm under the climbing sun.

Then this varied richness began slowly to fall away, and we entered a narrow valley which soon closed us within hills crumpled and bent by the ages. Now rocky outposts poked like bare knuckles through the thinning grass; trees became stunted and wind-twisted grotesques; drystone fences replaced the thick hedgerows; and there was only an occasional distant wisp of smoke to mark some small cluster of poor farm dwellings.

Through such sights we slowly climbed to the Nightsead village, a small huddle of sagging buildings situated where a large crack split wide the hard hills. Now when we stepped from the train, the air was noticeably cooler, and there was what I can only call a thinness to the gusting breeze that swept down from those barren slopes and along the single street of worn grey stone. Poverty was on that wind and was writ large, too, in the dispirited gaze of the few inhabitants in evidence.

Standing near the train platform was a dilapidated cart hitched to a bony old horse; with their shabby and avaricious owner Mr. Moseley bargained for transport to Nightsead. We left the village only to enter a rock treadmill that wound relentlessly up the side of the hills, following the path of a fast-flowing stream that we could always hear though seldom see. Then we had rounded the last curve, and the steep slopes that had enclosed us abruptly ended in an uneven field that slanted off to where, far to the right, some low dwellings announced a distant farm. Above us, to our left, bare and black was Nightsead.

What can I say to convey the stunning sight, the menacing air, the heavy oppression to the human soul of the ruins of Nightsead? Think of the Old Hall of Gainsborough, but cast it in the thickest, heaviest grey stone of the Tower, add to it the brooding hostility of Warwick Castle, and you will know something of the impression made by Nightsead.

Two monstrous rectangular structures there were, the first some seventy feet long, forty wide and at least fifty high, with no door evident from the top of that winding road from the village, with narrow arched windows set a good ten feet above the ground: cold and forbidding, it seemed designed to house some power greater than man's feeble spirit. Set at right angles at the far end of it, so close that the two shapes blended, was a smaller and lower building also of rock, sprawled out like a grim grey beast, with two huge wooden doors the only break in the solid wall of stone facing us.

More bewildering yet, on what would have been the third side of the square thus formed was a massive pile of rock, a veritable graveyard of stone from mere rubble at its outer edges to blocks half a man's height near the centre, all tumbled, scattered, blackened. What challenge had the power of Nightsead once mounted? What greater force had risen to bring her to this fragmented doom?

The cart had stopped in the very shadows of those mighty rock walls, Mr. Moseley began fishing out the promised few shillings of the fare, Aleck sullenly jumped down, bag in hand, and turned to reach for one of his several boxes.

"Aleck," I mumbled, "you can't live *here*, surely?"

His words, hard and bitter, were thrown over his shoulder. "I don't seem to have much choice, do I?"

"But . . . you live *here*?" I waved a helpless hand.

"This is Nightsead."

"But . . . that pile of fallen rock—why, there must once have been just as big a structure as that . . . that hall, to account for so much rock. What was the place ever built for?"

"I've no idea," Aleck replied shortly. Then, as if aware of his rudeness (caused, I am sure, by exhaustion), he added, "No one can tell you a thing about Nightsead, Jack. It simply exists, and that's all there is to it."

I took a box from him and reached for another. "The people of the area know nothing?"

"They'll tell you that Nightsead was once a great castle built by Sir Walter Raleigh. If you ask them the source of their information, they'll say that their father—or grandfather—said so."

"And that, to the country mind, constitutes proof." Mr. Moseley, having settled with the cart's driver, now came up, his own bag in one hand.

"At least there is no proof of anything else," Aleck replied sharply.

Mr. Moseley had been about to take up one of Aleck's boxes, but at this rude rejoinder he turned on his heel and strode off, quickly disappearing around the near corner that loomed above. With a sullen shrug Aleck followed, and I in embarrassed silence stumbled along behind him.

As we rounded that huge corner I could see that the only entrances to that monstrous hall were two doors, fashioned like those of the smaller structure of some rough, axe-hewn wood, dark as pitch and held in place by black iron strap-hinges. The one nearest to us was double, each panel a good four feet wide; the other, near the far end, was half the size. A thin path skirted that massive rubble heap and led to the smaller building; there we were apparently headed.

It was not until we had nearly reached this destination that I became aware that our approach was being watched. The path wound around the building, and on it a woman stood as silent and still as rock herself, a woman of tall, spare frame, with greying dark hair pulled back into an uncompromising bun, dressed in some dark material with a plain white apron her only adornment.

"Sae ye're back, sir," she observed in a quiet voice to Mr. Moseley who had now reached that smaller building.

With the barest of glances and the shortest of nods, he unlocked the second of the two doors and quickly vanished within, shutting the door behind him with a hard snap.

"Yes, we're back, Janet." Aleck's greeting to the woman was surprisingly warm. "This is my friend from

[25]

London, Mr. Watson. He is going to spend the summer with us."

"Aye? I took the hot water tae your room when I heard the bit cart. Ye'll mind that it will nae stay hot lang."

"We'll hurry," Aleck promised and pulled open the first door.

We stepped into a nearly bare stone box some twenty feet square, with heavy corner pillars meeting in a boss as plain as a soup plate and a pair of very high recessed windows in the far wall. At our left a small hearth had apparently been forced into the blocks at a date later than that of the original construction, for the very edges of the opening were rough-hewn and chipped. There, for all its crudeness, a small fire burned cheerily, and mighty welcome it was to me, caught in the desolate strangeness of that massive place. To the right was a heavy wooden door now stoutly boarded up and leading, Aleck said, to his stepfather's adjacent quarters. The chief furnishings of Aleck's room were a wardrobe and an old half-tester bed, and the only decoration a small framed photograph of a woman and child hanging on its headboard.

Aleck had lit a candle and now held it up to the picture. "That was my mother. I imagine that she was thought quite pretty."

Pretty she certainly was, though, in my poor opinion, overly dressed in a wide and feathered hat and much flowing drapery, with a decidedly bridal bouquet raised coquettishly in one hand. At her left was a tiny lad who was most obviously a young Aleck, but whatever had been on her other side was simply no longer there: the picture had been cut right through, and a blank piece of paper fitted into the space in the frame. Aleck gave no explanation, merely turning away to put the candle on the dressing-stand, and I made haste to follow him in using Janet's hot water to remove the worst of the travel grime.

Our brief toilet finished, Aleck led me out, past his stepfather's room, and around the far corner of the building. There, set back, was another stone structure, but what a contrast! A cottage, small and low, with a common deal door and shining square windows framed in simple white curtains.

Inside was a sight even more welcoming: a wide hearth with a glowing fire, a worn drugget before it, old chairs and a lamp or two, and in the middle a gate-legged table covered with a snowy cloth and laid for supper. There Mr. Moseley soon joined us, and Janet, coming in from her kitchen quarters at the rear, served as hearty a plain meal as weary travellers could wish. Even Aleck, I was delighted to see, ate hungrily, bringing a small smile to Janet's dour face as she carried in innumerable fresh pots of tea.

Yet throughout our light repast Aleck's cold manner to his stepfather remained unchanged, and I was secretly much relieved when, the meal ended, Aleck suggested that he and I return to our room. Once outside, however, he insisted that I at once meet the "guiding spirit of Nightsead" (this said with an unexpected twinkle in his hazel eyes), and, candle in hand, he led the way back to that massive hall of cold stone and flung wide those double doors.

A bright moon was rising, and so my first glimpse of that vast interior was touched by an eerie light that seemed only to deepen the dark that was all around us. Wide pillars, as plain as icicles, fanned out into the blackness above; the windows, even their lower sills higher than our heads, were shadowed rectangles buried in the depths of the walls. As we slowly walked down that huge and bare cavern, our footsteps made tiny drops of sound that raised faint ghosts of echoes, and I shivered—with the chill, at the strangeness, because of I know not what. Dimly at the far end I could make out a huge platform of stone, running right from one side to the other, with a gigantic black hearth behind it, and up those steps and across that expanse Aleck led me. Then, throwing me a quizzical grin, he raised his candle high.

What I expected to see I would have found it hard to say; I don't think that the blank grimace of a skull would have much surprised me. What was in truth revealed in that tiny, flickering light was a small frog nestled in bulrushes which rested on a single wavy line, all carved in the centre stone above the hearth. Both the little animal and his surroundings were so cunningly contrived that, as Aleck slowly moved the candle back and forth, the shifting flame seemed to bring a lifelike glow to those goggling stone eyes and to waft a swaying breeze across the rigidity of the rock bulrushes.

[28]

I found that, in relief as much as amusement, I had laughed aloud. Aleck joined me and, still laughing, we retired.

So began my Nightsead summer, a summer that turned out to be a surprisingly carefree time.

There was little enough for us to do around those stone buildings; hence, once we had given Janet whatever assistance she would accept with the simple chores of the place, we would turn gypsy and head out onto the swarthy slopes. Often Aleck and I were up and on the tramp while the dawn was still in the sky, returning to cross the deep stream at the bottom of the Nightsead hill only when the summer sunset was turning our chamber windows to fire. Many a meal we had in some distant farmhouse, or in a homely little inn reeking of smoke and beer; many a meal too was only a package of Janet's griddle cakes and a drink from the wandering stream. Whatever our fare and habits, however, Aleck soon looked his old self, and I never felt better, soon whistling light-heartedly on the way past that looming hall of stone and tumbling into bed at night with never a haunted thought.

Repeatedly while on our excursions I engaged the country folk in talk, trying to satisfy my curiosity about the history of Nightsead, but it was as Aleck had said: the people of the area knew nothing, although they were united in their belief that the tumbled ruins had once formed the castle home of Sir Walter Raleigh. That Sir Walter had entertained Queen Elizabeth at Nightsead was taken as a matter of course, and that the good queen had slept in Aleck's old half-tester (a gimcrack thing of brass which might at the most have been fifty years old) was declared next to "certain sure." Nor were the few gentry—the physician Dr. Leckie, the old vicar, and the village lawyer Mr. Roundtree—any more informative; all were comparative newcomers to the area, and all simply accepted Nightsead as part of the wild strangeness of the hills.

Often I would steel myself to wander into that massive cavern of a hall and gaze around me at those silent, blank stones, but all that I could ever deduce about the original purpose of the place was the obvious one of defense. Often too I climbed onto the wide platform that ran right across the one end of the hall and stared up at that little carved frog perched so cheekily among his rocky bulrushes, but he never had any information to offer me. There was a curious little broken stair set under one of the windows near that wide dais, a stair that went nowhere, that seemed designed to go nowhere; I even climbed this and gazed around me with totally uncomprehending eyes. The country people, I concluded, had as much right to their beliefs concerning Nightsead as anyone. As Aleck said, Nightsead was Nightsead.

So isolated and crude was the place that I did greatly wonder why Janet chose to remain. Yet she not only did so, she seemed seldom to leave the rocky environs that enclosed her. "Has she no family or friends?" I once asked Aleck.

"Never heard of any relations," Aleck replied, "and the only people she has ever bothered with around here are the Thatchers; they have the farm you can see across the Nightsead field. As long as I can remember, Janet has occasionally announced that we'd have to get our own tea as she would be 'oot,' and she'd stride off to the Thatchers. I was always strictly forbidden to follow her, and the only time I did, just for sheer mischief, she caught me at once and said, as stern as any judge, that if I ever tried that trick again she would leave Nightsead for good. That settled the matter, believe me: I couldn't visualize Nightsead without Janet. Why, she even taught me to read and write."

"*Janet* did?"

Aleck nodded. "You see, when I was small I couldn't manage those hilly miles into the village, so I wasn't sent to school. (In fact, I only started after the vicar made a bit of fuss about it, when I was about ten.) I don't know why Janet ever bothered teaching me—she said that it was to keep me out from under her feet, and that could well be true—but teach me she did. Not that I had much to read, and I certainly arrived at school with considerably less knowledge than Dan Thatcher, and he's nearly five years my junior. He took the opportunity to tell me so on my first day, and I was miserably ashamed. Because, you see, it was true."

"Did the Thatcher lad have some older brothers for you to make chums of?"

"No, the rest of the family are younger. Dan isn't the Thatchers' son, you see; he's a nephew from up north somewhere. Anyway, Janet forbade my going over to the Thatchers—she said they had enough to do without bothering with me—so I never got really friendly even with Dan. In fact, I was rather a lonely sort of kid all around."

"But surely *all* your education wasn't from either Janet or the village school, Aleck?"

"It was, really, except that the schoolmaster, who was a fine old fellow, soon set me extra tasks and arranged too for me to have weekly sessions with the vicar. He was so short-sighted that he was nearly blind, but as kind and good a teacher as ever lost his spectacles. All in all, I didn't do so badly."

In such moods, with the summer sun warm on our faces and the hard slopes of the hills open to our wandering will, Aleck seemed ready to accept his past life philosophically enough and to ignore the apparent vacuum of his future. But once when the little village church lay in our way, he abruptly turned off and led me across to a low and grassy mound where, without a word, he knelt and began clearing away the bits of lichen that had overgrown the small stone. When we as silently left, the carved lettering gave its own mute summary of my poor friend's early life: "Edith Raleigh" now showed clearly, but "Beloved wife of Ivor Moseley" and the dates of birth and death had been left as they were, hardly discernible under the green and clinging growth.

Of the history of Aleck's family, I learned a little. His father had died (of a ruptured appendix) in France, and it was there that his mother had met and married Mr. Moseley. She soon became ill and wished to be in her own homeland, so the little family had journeyed to Nightsead.

"She wished to return to *Nightsead*?" I exclaimed, I admit rather tactlessly.

"She had never seen it, nor, as far as the villagers know, had my father. It was simply the only property left to her, and of course *he* had nothing." (In such context, *he* invariably meant Mr. Moseley.) "He brought her here, and he killed her."

"Aleck!"

"She died of pregnancy and typhoid, with no one but Janet to care for her."

"Tragic, but—"

In reply Aleck laid a surprisingly gentle hand on my arm, his invariable way of uniting an admission of his unreasonableness with a plea for understanding of it. And with me, at least, that mute gesture never failed.

As the days slid swiftly by, greatly did I fear the effect on Aleck of his being left at Nightsead with only his stepfather and Janet for companionship. Accordingly, near the end of my summer visit I tentatively suggested to Mr. Moseley that Aleck's regained health could easily be lost should he indeed be forced to remain at Nightsead or the village.

"*I* have had to confine my own desires to the narrow path dictated by our financial position," Mr. Moseley returned quietly, "and I am afraid that Aleck must learn to do the same. He is young enough to make some sort of life for himself reading law at Roundtree's, and

I will somehow find the capital for him to do so, though I admit even that will be hard. More is impossible."

To this I could make no reply, for not only was there no sign of anything except the simplest of living at Nightsead, there was no evidence that Mr. Moseley had ever spent anything except the smallest sums on himself. Though he was always neat, his linen often gave indication of Janet's needle; the cut of his clothes was long out of fashion (indeed, one of his jackets was a virtual twin of a favourite of my father's during my childhood), and his only journeys, as far back as Aleck could remember, were occasional short trips into London, apparently to do with his own small income. As for his pleasures, these seemed to consist solely of his books—he spent nearly all his time in his own room—and of a weekly walk into the village to read Mr. Roundtree's copies of *The Times* (he obviously could not afford a subscription of his own). Certainly if Mr. Moseley could see only a narrow road ahead of his stepson, no one could accuse him of having had more himself.

Nor could I look for anything to come to my poor friend from his strange legacy. Loath to give up, I once broached the topic, and Aleck immediately stated frankly that, before his twenty-first birthday, he had himself had at least faint hopes of the letter's proving of some value, but that one quick reading had destroyed all such dreams.

"The letter is at least very old, is it not?" I was not ready to surrender the subject so easily.

"Oh yes, it's genuine Elizabethan. At least, the paper is."

"How can you tell?"

"There was a blank corner which had been bent back and nearly torn through. I removed it, and either the lawyer's clerk didn't notice or didn't care; at any rate he said nothing. I tracked down an expert at the B.M., and he assured me that the paper *is* Elizabethan. Of course that in itself means nothing."

"The letter couldn't be from Sir Walter Raleigh after all?" I still urged, I hardly know why.

Aleck laughed at my insistence. "No, it couldn't: the handwriting bears no resemblance to his, that much I do know. You'll have to forget the letter, Jack, as I've had to do: it's nothing but an historic oddity."

"Then why has it been kept so carefully?" I demanded.

"To make it an oddity, of course," Aleck replied with a grin.

And who knows, perhaps he was right.

Then one day near the end of that summer, Aleck abruptly disappeared for an afternoon, and when he returned told me that he would himself be back in London within the year.

"Oh yes, I will," he replied to my look of incredulity. "You have convinced me of one thing, Jack: that whether my stepfather truly can't, or whether he won't, continue to give me a small allowance is really immaterial. Either way, it is quite clear that I can expect no further help from him, and I know that I lack any legal means of redress. So be it.

"He keeps harping on my reading law at Roundtree's. Well, I've just been to see old Roundtree, and he is indeed in need of some assistance: he's the only lawyer now in this part of the county. So I am starting in his office, not to read law, which would cost my stepfather some money, but to work as a humble clerk, which will earn me a little. I shall save as much of my pittance as I can, and soon I shall be back in London, with my shillings in my pocket and enough experience in my head to enable me to find some low position there. My own studies will have to be confined to evening and Sunday hours, but whatever time I have will be forever free of my stepfather's damn interference."

Though I applauded Aleck's decision, I did wonder if his nervous structure was such that he could endure the daily drudgery of a village law office. I should not have doubted him: once his mind was made up, Aleck was iron within and steel without.

Although I must admit, as he later laughingly did, that his labours for Mr. Roundtree were much lightened by his increasing friendship with the young American, Miss Winnifred Hepworth, who came near the end of that summer to lodge for some weeks at the lawyer's house.

This young lady had until recently lived all her life in the United States, but as her father had been a traveller for some commercial firm, and as she and her mother had always journeyed with him, she had neither fixed abode nor close friends in her homeland, and the recent death of both her parents had left her singularly alone in the world and far from well provided for. What would have frightened many young ladies was to Miss Hepworth a challenge, and to her, true American that she was, a challenge existed only to be overcome.

She had been brought up to love English literature and to be remarkably well versed in it; hence, once she had her own way to make, nothing would do but she must make her new life in England. She had journeyed all by herself to London, had there found a position as lady's companion to an eminently respectable elderly lady, and had recently accompanied her employer to visit a relative in the Lake District. Her services not being further needed for some weeks, Miss Hepworth determined to see something more of the English countryside, and so had come by train to the village. Once there, she had applied to the vicar for a possible temporary lodging place, and so had become a paying guest at the Roundtrees'. Indeed, Mrs. Roundtree quickly became so fond of the bright-mannered young girl that Miss Hepworth was soon quite on family terms, and could be found as readily making early morning tea for the wife as spending an evening writing letters for the husband.

No doubt in such an isolated area, one moreover in which the few people of culture happened to be decidedly older, it was only natural that Aleck and Miss Hepworth should have been much thrown together. I am at least sure that no little gathering in the village was organized for the visitor's entertainment without Aleck's being automatically included. I am equally sure that soon all the district was noting with pleasure that there was no one whom Aleck would rather meet than Mrs. Roundtree's lodger, and no caller more welcome to Miss Hepworth than Mr. Moseley's stepson.

I knew nothing of this at the time, for in the nature of young men busy making their own way in the world, Aleck and I had exchanged no more than a brief note since I left Nightsead in the late summer. Then, in early December, I received an invitation from Aleck, with a few warm words enclosed from his stepfather, inviting me to spend Christmas with them. In his typically jesting fashion, Aleck wrote, "Come and wish Sir Froggy of the Hearth the compliments of the season, Jack."

I had nowhere in particular to go for the holidays and, rather wondering at my own temerity, accepted. In due time I arrived at the village and was met by Aleck driving an old dogcart and a sturdy little cob borrowed from the Roundtrees.

It was on that drive from the village that I first heard of Miss Hepworth, and by the time we arrived at Nightsead, I had become convinced that she was rapidly becoming the pole-star of my friend's existence. Aleck, I believe, had a most affectionate nature that had been thwarted by the loneliness of his childhood home. Now that his heart was given, it was given completely.

What Mr. Moseley would think of his stepson's attentions to the young American girl, I much wondered.

I soon had my curiosity satisfied, for that very first evening, while he and I were alone before a roaring fire (Aleck was returning the cob and cart and Janet was in her kitchen quarters), Mr. Moseley frankly told me that he was delighted with the growing intimacy of the two young people. He said that Aleck had not yet accepted the fact that he must turn seriously to a profession, and that his interest in Miss Hepworth could be a steadying guide. "A wife and family can be a very sobering influence on a young man, Mr. Watson."

While agreeing, I ventured to state my concern that Aleck would be unable for quite some years to support the wife and family which his stepfather was so readily anticipating for him. And as Miss Hepworth had herself been forced to take a position as lady's companion, she most probably was without—

"She hasn't a penny," Mr. Moseley at once agreed. "Or, as no doubt I should say, not a cent! But she has what is of much greater worth, Mr. Watson, and that is her woman's heart. *That*, as I know, can be a treasure of incalculable worth, and if my son is the fellow I think him, he will govern himself accordingly."

My own doubts subsided as soon as I was introduced to Miss Hepworth, for a more charming and at the same time forthright young lady I have never had the pleasure of meeting. Tall and slender, with black hair wound into a heavy twist on her neck, with firm mouth and round little chin and two of the merriest and, withal, shrewdest blue eyes that ever sized you up in an instant, she was totally delightful. What was more, she was a quick and independent thinker, had taken up Aleck's interest in the Elizabethans with a sharp intelligence which was little less than astonishing, and, under Aleck's amused gaze, had thoroughly explored the old Nightsead hall, even to climbing up that broken stair and smudging her shapely fingers with a close examination of that little stone frog. Naturally she soon ferreted out all the details that Aleck could give her concerning the strange Raleigh legacy and was vehement in urging him to pursue the mystery.

I can see her yet, sitting bolt upright in the Roundtrees' parlour, her hands clasped passionately and her blue eyes flashing as she declaimed, "I wouldn't sit down under it, Mr. Raleigh. I wouldn't!"

And I can see Aleck asking her teasingly just what she would do about the legacy.

"I'd find out the truth," Miss Hepworth replied at once. "No, I don't know how, but I would, Mr. Raleigh. I would indeed."

Though I joined Aleck in his hearty laugh, I could almost believe her.

Certainly we three young people took merry part in all the festivities in the village (Miss Hepworth played Father Christmas in the pageant to the astonishment of us all), and, fortified by hot toddy, Aleck and I fairly frisked over the miles to Nightsead. All in all, I was more than sorry when my few days of vacation were over, and I had to return to London.

I had one note, perhaps two, from Aleck during the next few months, in which, even in a scant page (about the length of our usual communications), his growing love for Miss Hepworth, who had of course returned with her employer to London, was made abundantly clear. Then, one day in late spring, my landlady informed me that a "Mrs. Raleigh" was below in the parlour asking for me, and indeed there she was, Mrs. Raleigh now, Miss Hepworth no longer, and looking very happy with her change of condition.

"We would have asked you to our wedding," she greeted me, offering her hand with the frankest of smiles, "except that we knew how busy you are and what a brute of a journey it is to Nightsead. So I've come to ask you to take me out to tea instead, for I've ever such exciting news to tell you."

So she had. In fact, the way she had swept the obstacles out of Aleck's path with her own brisk determination left me quite breathless.

Under her firm insistence, Aleck had asked Mr. Roundtree's help in finding a minor post in a London law firm, and this Mr. Roundtree had been able to do. Winnie—as over our tête-à-tête in the tea-shop she insisted that I must thereafter call her—had that very day come to London to find them lodgings.

"They're in a real hole, in a basement," she told me with the blithest of smiles, "but cheap and close to the British Museum so that Aleck will be able to go on with his studies. Now, Doctor Jack" (a name she had bestowed on me at Christmas), "I know what you're thinking: that we can't live on what Aleck will earn. But we can: I'm not a Yankee for nothing! And, what's more,

I feel sure that not only is Aleck's work on the Elizabethan poets important, some of it is worthy of print right now, and I know where to find those who can help him."

As indeed she did, for her former employer was herself connected by family with some of the leading journals, and she had willingly agreed to provide Aleck with introductions not only to editors but to other scholars working in the Elizabethan field.

"Since our marriage, we've been staying with Mr. and Mrs. Roundtree," Winnie wound up, "but we're moving to our new home this week. Now take me to the train, Doctor Jack, for Aleck will be fretting if I miss it."

At the station I asked her what Mr. Moseley thought of Aleck and Winnie's plans.

Winnie laughed. "I'm sure he *thinks* nothing because he *knows* nothing. Oh, of course he was at our wedding, but we haven't yet told him that we're not going to stay in the village."

"Why not?" I asked, much surprised.

"Well, we've only just finished arranging things. And . . . oh, I don't know. Because we haven't wanted to !"

And with her charming laugh, she was gone.

I was so busy with the completion of my own studies that I was able to visit my young friends only once before I left England for India. I must admit that I was shocked at the conditions under which they were living, in two small, dungeon-like rooms, poorly and scantily furnished, with tiny windows from which the total view seemed to be of the boots of passers-by. And of a couple of dustbins.

Yet, looking from Winnie's smiling face to the glow of deep content in Aleck's hazel eyes, I felt those dingy chambers to be better than many a gorgeous palace, and the litter of books and papers over seemingly every flat surface to be of very small moment indeed. And when I thought of the rocky vastness of Nightstead, in the midst of which Mr. Moseley would now be living alone with the dour Janet shut up in her cottage, I did not doubt that my friend had ahead of him the far better life. In the heart of the gallant, if penniless, young American girl, the descendant of Sir Walter Raleigh and the inheritor of his mysterious legacy had truly found a treasure of incalculable worth.

THUS ran the account of Nightsead and its inhabitants that I had left with Holmes the night before. So tired had I been when I retired that it was only in the morning that I remembered the paper which Mr. Moseley had left, calling it the crux of the whole legacy problem. Though Holmes had disparaged it, I had high hopes that it would indeed reveal something vital and, dressing quickly, hurried out to our sitting-room.

There, under the Persian slipper on the mantelpiece, was a folded sheet. Opening this, I found to my astonishment that the paper was headed in cursive block letters, "Copy of the Raleigh Letter." I read:

A last bless you. The father has much wronged me, though the son has done what he can, and for that we must be thankful. Poor royal fool, he is likely to suffer as my dear mort lord whose lips I yet kiss. May our two hearts stay as they are, and at the last put my great treasure there also. You did ever do what you believed right, and he was ever with God. I think often of when we were children and so sign myself as we did then.

But there was no signature at the end of the letter.

I sat and stared at the paper for many moments. So this was Aleck's legacy!—no wonder he had said that it seemed of no commercial value. What in heaven's name did the letter mean?

Who was the father who had wronged the writer, who the son, the "poor royal fool" who had done something to help and who was likely to suffer as "my dear mort lord"? What did "mort" mean? "Dead" seemed the obvious guess, but that could not be correct since the writer could still exchange a caress with the lord. At least the letter did mention treasure, even "great treasure"; unfortunately the only description of its whereabouts was incomprehensible. It was to be put "there" —*where*? The letter's recipient was of high morals, as was "he"—*who*? Were writer and recipient related, since they apparently shared childhood memories? Why could the letter not have had a signature, or at least the name of the one for whom it was intended!

All day I pored over this infuriating document and was accordingly bursting with questions when Holmes returned, which he did not do until evening.

"This letter, Holmes," I at once began.

"Near worthless, is it not?" he replied carelessly, seating himself at the table and taking up his napkin with every sign of an excellent appetite.

"But you must have *some* thoughts about it," I objected, pulling up my chair more slowly.

"At the moment," said he, raising the cover of the dish before him, "I find this excellent capon a much more satisfactory subject. What have you there, doctor?"

"Summer cabbage," I replied, more than a little shortly.

"Capital. Allow me to help you to bread sauce."

"That letter, Holmes—"

"Hardly worth interrupting a supper for, I assure you."

"Why are you so certain? Of course it is only a copy—"

"Which raises a most interesting question: how was it made? Remember that the terms of the legacy forbid the letter's removal from the care of the lawyers."

"Aleck could have made the copy from memory," I suggested.

"At least I am sure that he did not make *this* copy," Holmes replied, wielding a liberal spoon on the dressing, "for on his twenty-first birthday, immediately after seeing the original of the letter, Mr. Raleigh virtually admitted that it was both addressed to someone and in some way signed: the copy has no indication of either, and it is inexplicable that Mr. Raleigh would inadvertently omit such important details. More, this so-called copy is composed in wording and spelling of modern time: it is inconceivable that anyone as well-read in the original writing of the Elizabethan era as Mr. Raleigh could possibly be fooled by it."

"Perhaps Aleck *did* know that the letter was not genuine," I suggested, though much downcast at the thought, "and merely did not wish to admit it."

"His manner on the evening of his birthday argues against that. That is, of course, if your account is accurate."

"I would take my oath that it is."

"And I would accept your oath, for you have ever shown a good memory for facts. (If you observed them in the first place, that is.) It is therefore interesting that Mr. Moseley did not mention the name of his stepson, indeed did not say to whom the Raleigh legacy was to go. I think that we must assume that, for whatever reason, Mr. Moseley is trying to investigate the mystery without his stepson's knowledge."

"That could well be," I conceded, "if their relations have not improved. Mr. Moseley, I am sure, would have done all he could to help Aleck, but Aleck would not have welcomed his assistance."

"No. As for the lawyers, they—"

"You have seen the lawyers who have the letter?" I exclaimed.

"Certainly. It was the obvious place to start."

"Mr. Moseley named the firm to you?"

"No, nor did I request him to. But, as I expected, though the legacy paper itself is kept most religiously secret by its legal guardians, its existence as an historic curiosity is well-known in the Inns of Court, and I had only to apply to my own legal man to obtain the name of the firm—Champernowne—and a letter of introduction to one of the partners. Of course neither he nor anyone else in the office has ever read the letter, yet there were certain facts which were freely communicated to me, there being no secrecy about them.

"One is that the present legal firm has not only been in existence for over a hundred years, but that it is a direct business descendant from other firms which do stretch back to Elizabethan times."

"That seems rather tenuous, Holmes," I complained.

"It is, yes. In fact, I would be prepared to abandon the whole investigation except . . ." Holmes paused. "By the way, the lawyers informed me that, should the line of direct heirs ever die out, the letter would go into the keeping of the Crown. They also said that they had had the same inquiry from Mr. Moseley even before he brought his new family to Nightsead some twenty years ago. Reassuring."

"I cannot see anything reassuring about it," I objected.

"No? I confess that without these terms I would feel forced to take steps which I most certainly do not wish to initiate at this point. The Champernownes had another interesting revelation for me: there have been two other inquirers after the letter. Early on the day of your friend's birthday, a man claiming to be Mr. Raleigh appeared at the office of the legal firm, asking to be shown his legacy."

"I cannot believe that it was Aleck," I exclaimed, "for I am sure that he did not even leave the house until afternoon."

"Certainly the Champernownes found the claimant's means of introduction unsatisfactory, these consisting of a few bills, receipts, and so on, and as well they had already received a letter from Mr. Raleigh stating that he would be at their office in the middle of the afternoon. So the first gentleman was turned away with a polite request that he provide better identification; promising to do so, he departed, and needless to say did not return."

"The firm has no idea who he was?"

"They think that some newspaper had heard that the heir would that day come into his curious legacy (its existence, as I have said, is quite well-known among members of the legal circle), and had sent a reporter to see if some scraps of faked paper and much charming audacity would gain a story."

"I suppose that such an explanation *is* possible," I said slowly.

"It is, but I am not inclined to accept it. The man was quite a large fellow, fat faced, with rather high-coloured cheeks, and both quietly dressed and well-mannered. The lawyers' staff do not recall his eye colour, but do remember that he kept his gloves on—strange when he had to take several small pieces of paper out of his pocket-book, is it not?"

I nodded. "For whatever purpose, the fellow was in disguise. But you said that there had been *two* other inquirers about the Raleigh letter, Holmes."

"There were. There is, however, no mystery concerning the identity of the other: it was Miss Hepworth."

"Impossible, Holmes!"

"Unless it was someone impersonating the young lady (with remarkable success), it most certainly was. Not only does the visitor answer the description you give of Miss Hepworth—tall, black-haired and blue-eyed, with an American accent—but she gave her own name. She explained that she had learned of the strange Raleigh legacy and was merely curious about this apparent historic oddity. The lawyers obliged by giving her the same information that they gave me, that which is common knowledge in the legal fraternity, and the young lady, apparently satisfied, thanked them and went away."

"I suppose Winnie could have thought that she might, somehow, stumble on some new fact," I said slowly, "and gone to the lawyers—"

"That could not have been her reasoning, Watson, for Miss Hepworth made her visit *before* she went to the village, therefore before she had even met Mr. Raleigh."

I was so astounded that I could make no answer.

"Would you be willing to renew your earlier intimacy with Mr. Raleigh and his wife, Watson?"

"I would already have done so," I returned, "except that I have no idea where they are now living. Shortly after I arrived back in England I tried to call on them, but they had been gone from those miserable basement rooms for some months, and had left no forwarding address. And not knowing on just what terms Aleck might now be with his stepfather, I hesitated about writing to Mr. Moseley myself."

"Very wise. You don't remember the name of the London firm where Mr. Raleigh was employed?"

I shook my head. "I doubt very much if I ever heard it."

"Or the name of the photographer who took that picture of Mr. Raleigh's mother?"

"Edouard La Croix," I promptly answered, "of Baccarat. That is printed in the bottom right corner of the photograph, though why I should recall the name I cannot say."

"The reason for your memory I will leave to you medical men to puzzle over," Holmes returned, jotting the name on his cuff with a satisfaction for which I could see no occasion, "the fact is quite sufficient for me. Tell me, doctor, how old would you say Mr. Raleigh's mother appeared to be in that bridal picture?"

"She was not very young, Holmes," I admitted. "I should say over forty, although Aleck was only a small child—not much more than two, I should say."

"And Mr. Moseley does not appear to be yet forty; therefore Mr. Raleigh's mother must have been many years older than her second husband. And the wedding took place at Baccarat . . ."

"Quite a popular continental spot, I believe."

"Also the centre of a thriving glass industry." Holmes slumped down in his chair and stared at the empty grate for many moments. Finally, still gazing directly ahead of him, he said, "I suppose you would not feel up to making that journey to Nightsead, Watson?"

"Certainly," I replied with considerable surprise,

"though I cannot see what purpose my going would serve. We know that Mr. Moseley is here in London, and it is surely unlikely that Aleck is now there."

"I agree. Since, however, Janet has apparently been at Nightsead for nearly two decades, you would probably find her at home."

"And you think that she would know Aleck's address?" I hadn't thought of this possibility.

"I think there may be considerably more to Janet than we yet know."

"Then I shall go tomorrow."

"Capital. In the meantime I shall drop a note to Mr. Moseley—kindly ring the bell, Watson, and ask Mrs. Hudson to send for a special messenger—to request that he not leave London for a few days as I may have important information for him very shortly. There. Now we have done all that we can for the moment."

So saying, Holmes took up his violin. Between the doleful musical complexities which were his choice that evening and the thickening fumes from the pipe which he took up at frequent intervals, I very shortly decided that the better course for me was to retire early.

On the *qui vive* as my nerves were, I woke a little after dawn and soon decided that, as there was a very early train to Reading, I might as well begin my journey at once. I was rewarded by better connections than I had previously encountered on that small and exasperating line, and ended at the village a little before noon.

Having resolved, rather than to try to hire a horse, to climb across the hills to Nightsead, I had tucked a package of sandwiches into my pocket and stopped to eat my simple meal by the fast-flowing stream at the bottom of the Nightsead hill. As I clambered up the bank again I suddenly caught sight of the tall figure of Janet, striding swiftly across the field above me, apparently heading towards the Thatchers' farm.

Delighted to think that my errand might be accomplished so readily, I was about to hail her when I realized with a shock that there was a man half hidden in the bushes around the stream at the farther side of the field. His age I could not guess, beyond that indicated by his considerable height and general impression of vigour; as for his clothing, it appeared to be the moleskin trousers and vest, cotton shirt and heavy boots of the area's labourers, with a cap pulled down low on his forehead. What impressed me was the man's unnatural stillness and the steady gaze that he seemed to have fixed on Janet.

I had come to a halt, but apparently some slight movement of mine attracted her attention, for she abruptly stopped and half turned. For a moment she stood so, staring, stiffly arrested, and then as abruptly wheeled and started marching swiftly towards me. When I looked past her at the bushes across the field, the man had vanished.

Feeling more than a little awkward, I called out as cheerfully as I could, "Well, Janet, do you remember me?"

"Aye." Her face remained disinterested. "Ye're Mr. Aleck's friend, the one his wee wifey calls Doctor Jack. But by the pale look of ye," she had come right up to me by then, "your doctorin' has nae done ye over much guid yoursel'."

"You're right," I conceded. "I was serving in the army in India when I was wounded."

" 'Tis a fair pity when a man's got tae blow other men up for nae use at all." Having made this dour comment on the glories of empire, she stood silent, her hands tucked under her white apron.

I was finding it hard to begin. "Janet," I said hesitantly, "there was a man standing in those bushes across the field, and I'm sure he was watching you."

"Aye?" Her tone seemed completely indifferent. " 'T'would be one o' the farm laddies, and nae harm tae him at all. But what brings ye back tae Nightsead, doctor?"

"I was in the area," I felt compelled to lie, "and came to see if I could obtain Aleck and Winnie's new London address."

"Ye'll nae find the master at hame richt noo," Janet said (of course not to my surprise), "but I can tell ye where Mr. Aleck and Mistress Raleigh are noo stayin.' " Which she at once did.

Refusing her offer of a cup of tea, I started back to the village and the long train ride to London. I arrived at Baker Street late that evening, utterly exhausted.

Holmes was waiting up for me. He heard my account without comment, only asking at its conclusion, "Do you plan to call on Mr. and Mrs. Raleigh tomorrow, Watson?"

"I do, yes."

"Then, my dear doctor, be a receiver rather than a giver of verbal goods: do not inform them of our joint quarters, or of Mr. Moseley's visit to me. And now good night."

The next evening I searched out my friends, and found them in lodgings which, while very modest chambers just off Theobald's Road, were an infinite improvement on their old quarters. More, both were obviously in the best of spirits and delighted to see me.

"You have just missed Mr. Moseley," Winnie informed me as she took my hat and stick.

"You are on visiting terms, then?" I asked hesitantly.

Aleck laughed. "Apparently. We haven't been back to Nightsead, but he always calls when he's in London, and that seems to be quite often. And this time he arrived just when I was so bursting with my latest discovery that I was glad to have someone new with whom to share it."

"Then share it again with me," I urged.

"Sir Walter and Lady Raleigh's first child, who has always been thought to have died in infancy, survived. That is important because he could well be my ancestor."

"Oh, there's lots more," Winnie interjected, her blue eyes shining. "You've no idea how successful Aleck has been, Doctor Jack."

Though Aleck insisted that this was a great exaggeration, I think that Winnie was quite correct: not only had Aleck had several articles on the Elizabethan poets published in scholarly magazines, he had recently been commissioned to write a biographical introduction to a new edition of Sir Walter Raleigh's poems, and was accordingly now limiting his own literary studies to that great Elizabethan.

"And will the legacy letter be mentioned in the biography?" I asked eagerly.

"The publisher would very much like it to be," Aleck returned, "and for me to be able to prove my descent from Sir Walter—in fact, I have been given the commission with precisely that hope, for naturally any such reference would help the sales of the book. That's why I've been working so hard—and Winnie too, for she looks up all my references for me—on the Raleigh history. Now, Jack, what's been happening to you? for it's obvious that something has."

I was soon deep in recounting my war experiences to an audience as interested as any returned soldier could desire, and it was late when I returned to Baker Street. Holmes, however, was still up (indeed, I had the distinct feeling that he had been waiting for me) and listened intently to all that I could tell him.

"Aleck appears in excellent health," I concluded.

"Whatever caused that early illness of his seems to be troubling him no more."

"Tell me, Watson, this doctor whom Mr. Raleigh saw at that time, Abernathy: how would you rate his competence?"

"Adequate for routine matters, at least when he was younger. He died while I was in India."

"A pity, for there is something about that sudden attack of sickness after Mr. Raleigh's birthday supper ... Are you sure of the placement of the pieces of the lamp that Mr. Raleigh knocked to the floor when he was taken ill?" Holmes took up my manuscript from the table and read out what I had written. " 'Bits of the chimney and pieces of the bowl were nearly under Aleck's feet, and the burner had rolled half-way across the room'? Are you sure of that?"

"I would not have written so if I had not been," I replied.

"Curious," Holmes remarked, rising to his feet. "Good night, doctor."

"I shall be away for a day or two, Watson," Holmes announced next morning. "Keep any messages that come for me, if you will be so good."

"Shall I forward your mail?" I asked.

Holmes shook his head. "I will be back very soon."

However, he was away the better part of a week, and when he returned there was a note from Mr. Moseley awaiting him.

"What do you make of this, Watson? Mr. Moseley has asked that I return the copy of the Raleigh letter to him."

"His reason?" I asked in surprise.

"That since has has not heard further from me, he has decided to abandon the inquiry as one that cannot be profitably continued. He also most courteously asks me to present my bill."

"You are sending the letter back?"

"Certainly. And will refuse to submit any bill."

"Since your communication with Mr. Moseley seems to have ended, do you not wish to meet Aleck?" I asked hopefully.

"I can see no purpose in it."

"You are dropping the case," I concluded, much downcast.

"Far from it. In fact, doctor, you may recall that earlier I said that I was not convinced that the Raleigh legacy could be called my case. I say that no longer."

"But if Mr. Moseley no longer wishes to engage you—"

"My services are required by someone else: by a blind lady who holds aloft a pair of scales. By the way, that address which Mr. Moseley gave me is an accommodation one. I have often used it myself."

"Why should Mr. Moseley do so?" I asked, puzzled.

"Obviously because he does not wish to reveal his true London residence. Why, I have no idea."

"If you are not going to see Mr. Moseley again, and will not meet Aleck—"

"Better say that Mr. Moseley does not care to see *me* again, and that *I* do not feel that meeting Mr. Raleigh—or Mrs. Raleigh—at the moment would do any good."

"I suppose you have no intention of telling me what you *are* going to do?" I returned, decidedly nettled.

"On the contrary, I was about to ask you to be my guide on a very private journey to Nightsead."

"To Nightsead! But why?"

"Because both its strange ruins and the strange legacy letter are in Mr. Raleigh's family. If some connection could be found between the two, something promising might result. I admit as well to being intrigued by your description of Nightsead."

I hastily pulled my thoughts together. "Mr. Moseley will be there, surely; he has no doubt remained in London merely in order to have your answer to his note."

"Which he will not have before tomorrow since I have not yet posted it," Holmes returned. "Mr. Moseley is therefore highly unlikely to be at Nightsead tonight."

"*Tonight?*"

"You are engaged?"

"Holmes, this is really . . . And in any case there is hardly likely to be a train."

"There is a good connection to Wrinehill," Holmes replied (he often seemed to carry a complete Bradshaw in his head), "the little town on the other side of the Nightsead hill, and I have wired the station-master to see if some kind of hired gig cannot be produced there. You *are* coming, doctor, are you not?"

Of course I was, and we were soon on the train. Indeed, I had soon settled into a lengthy doze, for Holmes was so uncommunicative that it was evident that he intended being alone with his thoughts. We alighted a couple of hours after midnight, and were met by the station-master himself, who had indeed procured a horse and trap for us.

"I couldn't find a driver, sir," he apologized, "for it's 'arvest time, and every man jack is out in the fields 'til 'e's ready to drop."

"No matter," Holmes replied, swinging up into the seat and taking the reins, "we shall do very well ourselves. Giddup, my lad!" And with that we were off.

I had often been surprised by the many skills which Holmes possessed, indeed seemingly any and all which his curious profession might require. This night was partly overcast, there was as well that low drifting mist which so often comes as the despair of the farmer, the roads which we drove over were often no more than country lanes and local byways, yet Holmes kept the horse at a comfortable trot and never hesitated to direct the animal on.

I once ventured to remark that Holmes might well be driving in Marylebone, so sure he seemed as to where we were going. "An amazing amount of information can be gathered from an ordnance map," he replied, "and I have spent several hours studying one of the largest scale that Stanford's stock. I shall be very surprised if we end very far from where I expect to be."

Indeed we did not: through ways that were utterly

strange to me, we wound around to the Nightsead hill.

"Now, Watson," Holmes had jumped down and was briskly tying up the horse, "should we fail to enter Nightscad without—"

"To enter! Holmes, I really cannot—"

"Most certainly: for what else have we come? Should we fail to enter without rousing Janet from her quarters, I shall have to vanish into the background and you to step forward with some plausible explanation for your presence. But I hope that we shall not be pressed to that expedient."

So most fervently did I, and most fervently too did I wonder at my assisting Holmes in this dubious enterprise. Only my confidence that we were, somehow, serving my friend's best interests kept me stumbling along at Holmes' side as we climbed the last long yards, the mists often obliterating our boottops and the dark lantern which Holmes had taken from his pocket casting a faint yellow glow before us.

Only once did we stop, when we had at last reached the top of the hill. As we paused, staring across at the deeper blackness against the sky that was Nightsead, the moon burst out of the drifting clouds, and at my side I heard Holmes catch his breath. Seen so, Nightsead was indeed awesome, more shadowed than lit, silent, blind, unyielding, with that smaller structure jutting out from its far end, dark and cold, with, too, that incredible pile of rock and rubble stretching far above a man's head in broken isolation across the hard earth.

Yet I was completely unprepared for Holmes' comment, whispered as it was to himself. "So I was right. A leading clue, and it lies there before us."

I knew better than to expect Holmes to answer any query of mine at such a moment, so in silence we climbed the last yards. Much I pondered, however, on what possible clue there could be in the very appearance of Nightsead, which, I would swear, I had described accurately in my manuscript. Whatever it was, it eluded me still.

Not until we reached the deeper shadows of the lintel of that massive double door to the old hall did we pause again, and then only for a moment. The moon had retreated into the clouds, the night remained dark and silent all around us, and Holmes quickly and softly eased open the door.

Once inside he strode down that cavernous emptiness without hesitation. Briefly we paused by that bit of stone stairway, and the light in Holmes' hands sprang up step by step to the broken top, and then we moved on to mount that wide dais.

Holmes at once darted over to the hearth, and began to play the lantern over that little carved frog. Certainly, though crudely cut, the small creature possessed a certain whimsical charm, but why Holmes should choose to spend several minutes—and at such a time!—examining it, even impatiently beckoning me forward to direct the lantern's light while he used both lens and fingers on and around the carving and at last polished off a bit of the grime of past years with his handkerchief, I could not understand.

Finally, and to my great relief, Holmes turned away, not back down the hall but to the smaller door at the side of the dais. A moment's pause at the bottom of the outside steps, and Holmes was moving on, across the corner of the rectangle to Aleck's door. This, as I could have told Holmes, was never locked, indeed could not be by the ancient hunk of iron which was the only mechanism on the door. However, we spent only a moment in my friend's room: one quick swing of the lantern's light, and Holmes led me out and on to the door of Mr. Moseley's chamber.

That, as always, was locked, but, to my astonishment, Holmes took from the deep pocket of his cloak a pair of peculiarly thin pincers and in a moment had the door open. Allowing for the architectural oddity of Nightsead, it seemed to me an ordinary enough chamber, large and gloomy with its massive stone walls reflected but dimly in the small light, furnished with bed, highboy, wardrobe, a desk in the corner and an easy chair by the wide hearth. Nearly distraught with unease at the compromising situation in which I found myself, I remained near the door, trespassing as little as I could.

Obviously no such scruple bothered Holmes. He began by making a quick search for something of apparently small size: his long fingers flickered rapidly through drawer and cupboard, under the bed, even under the mattress. All he found of any obvious interest was a gun, leaning against the back of the wardrobe, and a box of shells; I was quite startled, but Holmes gave them no more than a cursory glance and moved over to a small bookcase. There he worked with methodical quickness from side to side of each shelf, looking at every book with what I can only call thorough haste. Several times he even examined a page or two with his lens, though never taking more than a few seconds to do so.

At last, after a final survey of the room, he took up the lantern and led the way out.

We were not yet to leave Nightsead, however, for Holmes at once picked his way over to that massive pile of fallen rock and, to my utter astonishment, began to scramble up the stones until he had reached the jagged top. Here he stood and, the lantern fully open and held high, turned slowly from side to side, apparently intent on the extent and placement of those tumbled rocks. Only after some minutes (very long ones they seemed to me) did he climb down and in silence take us back to the twisting road.

Dawn was gilding the sky as we stumbled down the Nightsead hill, our muscles stiff with the morning chill.

"The Thatchers' farm is across the field?" Holmes asked, pausing at the bottom.

"It is. In fact, this field is part of their acreage, although it is too sloping and rocky for planting. That gun in Mr. Moseley's room—"

Holmes shrugged. "That shotgun? I think you would find some such weapon in most of the isolated farmhouses of the area. Did you never come across a farm lad out after rabbits or possibly a bird for the family dinner?"

I admitted that I had, and Holmes said no more.

Once we were back at the station-house, however, I pressed the question which was uppermost in my mind: what was it about Nightsead which Holmes had at once seen and which had completely eluded my much greater familiarity with that gigantic ruin?

"You saw Nightsead with your mind ready to view it as an ancient baronial dwelling, as a one-time home of Sir Walter Raleigh," Holmes returned, "I did not." Then, as I started to speak, "I have myself some answers yet to gather, doctor. When I have them, you shall hear all."

So I switched the subject to another point that was troubling me. "Wherever did you obtain that thin-jawed pair of pliers, Holmes?"

"From a burglar who was once a client of mine."

"You don't mean to say that you aided a guilty man!"

"Oh no, he was innocent . . . at least of the particular crime with which he had been charged. But he couldn't prove it because he refused to say what he had been doing at the time in question."

"And that was?"

"Eloping with his landlord's daughter."

"Surely a more harmless act than burglary," I suggested, laughing.

"Not at all. The reason he and his young woman were able to solemnize their union was because her father was nowhere to be found. And the new husband was much too fly a chap to be the cause of police inquiries into the activities of his father-in-law."

"You were able to prove the bridegroom's innocence on other grounds, I take it?"

"On the best grounds of all: by finding the real thief. He turned out to be not only a professional rival of my client, but himself a suitor of the girl. My chap was so grateful for his double triumph that he swore that he would pull a job the very night he was released in order to reward me. I persuaded him to allow me instead the pick of his tools. Ah, here at last is our train."

At that very early hour we had the carriage to ourselves, and so I at once renewed my questioning. "What were you looking for in Mr. Moseley's room, Holmes?"

"Something which I hardly expected to find, yet very much wish that I had. No, no more at this time, Watson; I could well be wrong. Although . . . if only your friend's mother had not been married at Baccarat!"

"Why did you examine Mr. Moseley's books so closely?"

"That is another subject, doctor, on which my deductions are not yet complete. When they are, you shall have them."

"And why did you want to look at that stone frog above the hearth? Are your deductions there also incomplete?"

"Decidedly. I examined the little creature because I did not understand it. And I frankly admit that I still do not."

What there was to understand about stone frogs I could not see and was about to say so when, turning, I found Holmes already stretched out, his cloak wrapped tightly around him, the smoke rising steadily from his pipe and the occasional quick gleams from those grey eyes speaking of a mind already at once distant and concentrated.

We made the rest of the journey in silence.

It was late the following afternoon before I climbed from my bed, and yet I rose still heavy with exhaustion and annoyed with myself for it. Once I could have worked at the hospital all day, studied half the night, and still sprung up refreshed and ready to begin the round again, but I had left too much of that youthful vigour in the pain and sickness of the Afghan Wars.

It was some comfort to find that Holmes too had slept late. Over our breakfast he casually asked if I had ever examined any of Aleck's old books of poetry. I shook my head.

"Will you be calling on the Raleighs this evening?" Holmes next asked.

"I am certainly willing to do so," I replied.

"Would you also be willing to remove one of Mr. Raleigh's books? I believe that you would be able to return it very shortly."

"Holmes, I am hardly in the habit of 'removing' a friend's possessions!"

"As you are unlikely to have had many friends in Mr. Raleigh's interesting position," Holmes replied drily, "an exception should be in order."

"In any case, which of Aleck's books do you want to see? I'm sure I don't remember a single title."

"All that matters is that it be one of the books which Mr. Moseley gave him."

With this strange commission, and with the private resolve that I would openly ask Aleck to lend me one of his books, that evening I set off to call upon my friends. My task was fortunately made easy by Aleck's being alone in their lodgings, and I was accordingly able to ask at once about his work on Sir Walter Raleigh.

Aleck's thin face lit with the glow of intense satisfaction. "I have been able to conclude a rough draft of the biographical sketch with a tracing of my family: there is no doubt, Jack, that I *am* a descendant of Sir Walter's first child."

I warmly congratulated my friend on the success of his research, and casually asked, "What first turned your thoughts so exclusively to the Elizabethan poets, Aleck? I suppose it was your possible connection with Sir Walter?"

For a moment my friend said nothing, then replied, "That's rather a sore subject with me. No, don't apologize, Jack: I don't mind telling *you*. You see, all those early years that I lived in isolation at Nightsead, alone with Janet and my stepfather, I thought that he was my true parent: certainly I addressed him so, and he never informed me otherwise. Then when I finally went to school, I discovered the truth—in fact, it was young Dan Thatcher who, pretty bluntly, told me that my name was not Moseley."

"That must have been quite a shock."

"It was. No doubt it would have been far worse if my true name had been other than what it is, but in that area the Raleighs of Nightsead are still automatically considered gentry. Even so, after my first day at school I tore home and had a royal row with my stepfather. He said that he had always intended telling me the truth when I was older and could understand better, and I suppose he may really have thought that he was doing the right thing. He told me then about the legacy letter too, although that didn't mean much to me at the time.

"I suppose, Jack," with one of his abrupt shrugs, "at heart I'm a queer fish. I know, while my stepfather was still trying to explain things to me, I slammed into my room, took down that picture over my bed, and cut him right out of it. Snip, snap, and he was gone and into the fire. And many a time through the years I've wished that he had never entered my mother's life.

"Though at the same time I must admit that he's been decent enough to me. The only time he gave me a hiding I suppose I deserved it: I'd gone without permission into his room and taken a book out of his case."

"That doesn't sound such a serious sin for a small boy," I protested.

"Well, I'd always been strictly forbidden to enter my stepfather's room, you see, and always before it had been locked; I'd hear the latch click home whenever the door was shut, and I knew it had to be opened with a key. But this time the door hadn't quite closed, and I couldn't resist the temptation: in I went.

"I don't think I would have done anything more than take a look around and sneak out again, except that I caught sight of a bookcase packed with books, and I had so few of my own. The first couple I grabbed were histories, and I soon put 'em back, but the next was poetry, and that finished me. I was still standing there, completely entranced, when my stepfather came in, and I really can't blame him for taking his belt to my rear end.

"Especially as he *did* shortly thereafter give me all the poetry books he had, about a dozen and all of the Elizabethans. And at least those books kept me out of any more mischief: thereafter I was either hunched up in some corner, reading, or tramping the fields to the rhythms I'd already packed into my head. I suppose I shouldn't feel the way I do towards my stepfather, but . . . Ah well, it doesn't matter now, does it? We're good enough friends these days."

At breakfast the next day I told all this to Holmes and gave him the book which I had openly borrowed from Aleck, an old copy of *Elizabethan Poets*. For the next few minutes Holmes was totally engrossed in a strangely careful inspection of the book.

"As I thought," he said at last, shutting the book and leaning back in his chair. "On our way home from Nightsead, you asked me what I was looking for in Mr. Moseley's small library, and I said that I would reveal my conclusions when I could do so fully. Light your pipe, doctor, for I am about to redeem my promise.

"All Mr. Moseley's books are on Elizabethan history."

"Without exception?"

"As far as the volumes in that bookcase go (and I would say that they constitute virtually all he owns), without exception."

"He at one time also owned a dozen books of Elizabethan poetry," I reminded Holmes, "for he gave those to Aleck."

"Quite so, a fact which I shall leave for the moment. The history books are all rather old: none has been printed for more than twenty years. All have had their flyleaves removed, 'Ivor Moseley' written on the inside cover, and many have short jottings in their margins— jottings which are not in Mr. Moseley's writing. More, these are of the kind traditionally made by the student: an outline of dates, names of important personages, summaries of events, and even that despairing piece of self-advice, 'Re-read.' I doubt that you have scribbled such notices in any book for a number of years, doctor, and I am also sure that, were I to look at some of your old university texts, I would find precisely such aids to a pre-examination cram in abundance."

Laughing, I agreed to both presumptions.

"Now we come to this book of poetry which you have borrowed from Mr. Raleigh. It too is well over twenty years of age, has no flyleaf, has 'Ivor Moseley' on the inside cover, this heavily blacked out, and your friend's name added. And it has no notes of any kind."

"I remember Aleck once saying that books were so precious to him that he could never bear to mark them in any way."

"That would explain why he has not written in this volume; it does not explain why the original owner did not, the owner who wrote those student notes in the history text."

"We do not know that there was a single owner," I objected.

"It is a reasonable supposition, I think, because of the common field of the Elizabethan period and the common ownership by Mr. Moseley. Let us say that the original buyer of the books was a student of Elizabethan history, a lover of Elizabethan poetry, and quite probably at university more than twenty years ago. That takes us some way to identifying him."

"Could it not be Mr. Moseley himself?"

"Not unless he attended university much more recently: five-and-twenty years ago he would have been only a youth. And if indeed he is the books' first owner, it is strange that there are no texts from later years. Then too there is the fact that the flyleaves have been removed from all the books. *All.*"

I waited for further revelations and waited in vain. "I suppose you have nothing further of importance to tell me," I finally suggested, with more than a touch of sarcasm.

"Very little," Holmes replied, totally unperturbed. "I will just commend to your memory the fact that the vicar of the Nightsead village is, according to Mr.

Raleigh (whom I have no reason to doubt on the question), so short-sighted as to be almost blind at any distance."

With that Holmes retired to his room.

When I woke the next morning and found the day lying boringly empty before me, found too that Holmes had once more gone out, I was suddenly struck with the idea of taking myself to the British Museum for some research of my own. No matter what Holmes said, I could not quite rid my mind of the belief that, though admittedly I could make little of it, that copy of the Raleigh letter had some importance: it did, after all, name treasure—even "great treasure." Perhaps a fresh eye could spot something in the Raleigh biographical material that would be revealing. At any rate, I had nothing better to do (I was waiting for answers to yet more inquiries I had made concerning medical practices), and so took up my hat and stick and headed for Bloomsbury.

Once inside the Reading Room, I was quickly and most courteously attended by a succession of those elderly and chalky-seeming gentlemen who appear to abound in the venerable institution of the B.M. and who seem able to track down any item of knowledge ever conceived by human brain. I had had no idea that the published references to Sir Walter Raleigh were so voluminous: there appeared to be no end to them! The faster I tried to skim the books put in front of me, the more bewildered I became; I tried to make notes but was forced to abandon that since I had no idea what was important to my search and what was not; the stuffy atmosphere of the crowded room was making my head swim; and I was soon in that state of nervous irritability which futile exhaustion readily produces.

Looking up from my desk to ease my tiring eyes, I was startled by the sight of a tall, reddish-bearded, florid and fat-faced man hastening towards the exit. For some seconds I stared stupidly after him, wondering why a man whom I was sure I had never seen before should yet seem so familiar. Then the kaleidoscopic pieces of my impression shifted into a startling picture: the man was the very incarnation of the fellow who had attempted to impersonate Aleck on the morning of his twenty-first birthday!

I sprang to my feet: too late. By the time I reached the end of the aisle, he was already entering the foyer; as I pushed my way out through a throng of people just entering, he disappeared from my sight. A quick journey around the streets adjacent to the Museum revealed nothing.

Naturally I was fully aware that there were, no doubt, a hundred or more men in London who would answer to just such a description, yet I was myself sure that this fat-faced fellow was Aleck's impersonator and that he was up to no good in the Reading Room. Feeling completely frustrated, I at last took a cab back to Baker Street, fervently hoping that Holmes was at home. He was not, but even as I flung my hat and stick down in despair, I heard his quick step on the stairs.

"You never appeared at a better time," I exclaimed.

"That is because I saw you flying along Oxford Street at a pace which meant a promised guinea at the least," Holmes replied, calmly seating himself, "so I thought that I had better return. Now, doctor, what caused your heels to sprout such sudden and expensive wings?"

I rapidly told him of the red-faced man whom I had seen at the Museum. "I know that you'll say that he could be one of countless others," I concluded.

Holmes' comment, however, was far different. "Tell me, Watson, could the *man* you saw have been a *woman* in disguise?"

For a moment I stared in astonishment. "You can't suspect Winnie!" I finally exclaimed in disbelief. "Why in heaven's name would she wear a disguise to go to the Reading Room?"

"So as not to be easily recognised by her husband should he drop in as he often does. And Mrs. Raleigh is, by your account, a tall young woman and able to act a part."

"Father Christmas in a village pageant," I agreed scornfully.

"For which she no doubt wore padded clothing and both beard and moustache. What tone of voice has Mrs. Raleigh?"

"Contralto," I admitted. "But, Holmes, why should Winnie mind if Aleck met her in the Reading Room? She is, after all, helping him with his research."

"Is she? Is she perhaps also engaged in doing some research of her own? Has she ever mentioned in your hearing her mother's maiden name, Watson?"

"Of course not. Why should she?"

"Because it too was Raleigh. If only as a striking coincidence, do you not think it strange that she has not told you? It would be interesting to know if she has informed her husband."

"I am sure that she has," I replied stoutly.

"Would you be willing to find out?"

I remained silent, not at all liking the implications of this.

"Remember, Watson, some months before she met Mr. Raleigh, Miss Hepworth not only knew of the legacy letter, but was curious enough to inquire about it. More, she knew where to ask her questions: she knew of the Champernownes. Then there is her visit to the village: you did not find anything strange in that?"

"Certainly not."

"Miss Hepworth reportedly came to England because of desire to see the country, yet, when her employer goes to visit the Lake District, Miss Hepworth chooses rather to make that difficult journey to the isolated village and bare hills of Nightsead. Do you really not find that strange, doctor?"

Put like that, I had to admit that I did.

"There is another point. Her former employer (whom I easily traced through the editors of the scholastic journals) has informed me that, while they were in

London, Miss Hepworth spent much of her free time at the British Museum and was openly enthusiastic about her readings in the Elizabethan period."

"But, Holmes . . ." I tried to pull my scattered thoughts together. "There can be no harm in Winnie's interest, no matter what first roused it: she cannot possibly profit from the Raleigh legacy herself. Except, of course, by marriage——" I stopped short.

"As you say. Though there is another way, Watson. I have checked with the lawyers: the heir to the legacy does not have to be male. So in her own right Mrs. Raleigh may have a claim through her mother and may be secretly investigating that claim. And of course if anything were to happen to Mr. Raleigh . . ."

"It is not possible," I exclaimed as soon as I could speak. "Winnie would never harm Aleck, never, not in any way, not even should that 'great treasure' be as fabulous as I hope and it lying right in front of her, hers for the taking."

To this Holmes made no reply, and it was I who retired to my room.

The next evening I returned from a solitary walk to find this scrawled note waiting for me.

Doctor Jack—
I beg you come at once to St. Bartholomew's Hospital—Aleck is *terribly* ill. Please, please hurry, I am nearly out of my mind.

Winnie

Holmes entered as I sprang up, read the note as I grabbed my hat and stick, and was at my heels as I ran down the stairs.

At the hospital, in the corridor outside the ward, we were met by Winnie and, to my surprise, by Mr. Moseley. Winnie, though she was very pale, had herself in the grip of an iron composure and acknowledged my introduction of Holmes with quiet courtesy. Not so Mr. Moseley: he looked corpse-like, he was so white, and was visibly trembling. He hardly seemed to know me, and, as for Holmes, he merely stared at him, with beads of sweat breaking out on his own forehead.

It was Winnie who told us what had happened. Late that afternoon, Mr. Moseley having come to London for a few days to see about some business matters, he had happened to meet Aleck on the street. Mr. Moseley was of course keenly interested in the progress of Aleck's research into the Raleigh biography and had ended the conversation by asking Aleck and Winnie both to dine with him.

Accordingly, the two men had returned to Aleck's lodgings, Winnie had joined them, and all three had gone to a little restaurant near Russell Street where, Mr. Moseley said, he had often himself eaten. The meal ordered, they were all eagerly discussing Aleck's latest research discovery when a sort of Gypsy fellow, who is apparently a regular employee of the place, began to wander from table to table playing a violin. Mr. Moseley beckoned to him and requested that he play some American songs for the young lady, which he did although his repertoire was decidedly limited.

He had hardly finished when Aleck had suddenly leaped to his feet, crying out that he was ill; he had almost immediately collapsed, clutching his abdomen and moaning with pain. He was assisted to a washroom where, Mr. Moseley said, he had been horribly sick, and, as Aleck's condition seemed if anything to be worsening, he had been brought as fast as a cab could be summoned to St. Bartholomew's.

"Why did you not go to St. Peter's?" I here interrupted. "Surely it is nearer to Russell Street?"

"I am afraid that it never came into my mind," Mr. Moseley replied frankly. "St. Bartholomew's was the only hospital I could think of, so I ordered the cab here."

"The doctor has said nothing yet?"

Winnie shook her head. "We haven't even seen him."

"You say that at the restaurant your meal had been ordered," Holmes questioned. "Had your husband eaten any part of it, Mrs. Raleigh?"

She again shook her head. "We were still waiting for the food. Aleck had had nothing but a little wine."

"And *that* couldn't have hurt him," Mr. Moseley here interjected, "for we all had a glass from the same bottle (it was a Beaune, which I have often seen Aleck drink), and it did no harm to either Winnie or myself."

"How much of his glass had Mr. Raleigh taken?" Holmes pressed.

"I should say about half," Winnie replied, "about the same as Mr. Moseley. I had had only a few sips, but, in any case, Mr. Holmes, neither of us is the slightest bit the worse for it. That wine *couldn't* have hurt Aleck."

"He had had nothing else to eat or drink at the table? Not a drink of water, a bite of a roll, nothing at all?"

"Nothing," Winnie said emphatically, adding, "there was nothing on the table that could be so much as swallowed, except for the wine."

"And there was nothing wrong with the wine," Mr. Moseley added desperately.

"I am not so sure," Holmes replied thoughtfully.

"But how could there have been?" Mr. Moseley exclaimed. "Winnie and I are fine, and I assure you that I at least had drunk as much as Aleck. And—why, how stupid of me! I have the rest of the bottle here." He was reaching for his overcoat which he had dropped onto a chair. "There was a terrible confusion at the restaurant, as you can imagine, with everyone trying to help and the proprietor wringing his hands in horror, and while we were waiting for the cab (which of course seemed to take hours to come), I suddenly remembered that I should pay for the wine and pressed some money into the proprietor's hand. He dashed off and came back with the bottle, saying that as I had paid for it I should have it. The cab came up then, and I just rammed the thing into my pocket. Here it is, Mr. Holmes."

It looked like a perfectly ordinary bottle of Beaune to me, and Holmes, pulling the cork, admitted that he could smell nothing wrong with the contents. "Do you wish it back, Mr. Moseley?"

"No, no," he said with a shudder. "I never want to see a bottle of Beaune again, and I'm sure Winnie does not."

"Not that bottle, at any rate," she agreed with an attempt at a smile, and so Holmes put it into his own pocket.

At that moment one of the doctors came out of the emergency room, and we all turned to him with that breathless interest which can only come at such moments. His news was so good that for a moment I stood stunned with relief: the illness had not returned, Aleck was conscious though exhausted, and, while he would most certainly have to remain in hospital at least overnight, he was apparently recovering well, as he had after that sudden attack of violent sickness on the evening of his twenty-first birthday.

At this point poor Winnie burst into tears, and while I was endeavouring to soothe her, I heard Holmes ask what had caused Aleck's illness.

"We really have no idea," the doctor replied. "There are no evident signs of disease—in fact, Mr. Raleigh appears to have been in excellent health—and as the worst of the attack was over before he reached the hospital, of course we have no intestinal matter to examine." With a little bow he returned to the ward.

Shortly thereafter Holmes announced that he would leave, saying that he could see no good that he could do at the hospital, and, rather to my surprise, Mr. Moseley also said that he would go. He shook my hand very warmly, patted Winnie on the shoulder, and, saying that he felt a new man (which indeed he looked), went out with Holmes.

Winnie and I spent the rest of the night in the waiting room. A couple of times we were permitted to tiptoe in to look at Aleck, who was sleeping soundly and apparently in no discomfort, and in the morning we had the great joy of seeing him, though understandably exhausted, clear-eyed and consuming weak tea and dry toast with no sign of harm.

Having first insisted upon Winnie's joining me for breakfast, I saw her safely back to the lodging-house and went on to Baker Street.

I found Holmes, his long legs stretched out, his elbows on the arms of his chair, his fingertips placed neatly together, and the air as blue as his dressing-gown—all signs that I well knew betokened a period of intense thought. Moreover, though upon my entering he roused himself to give his customary courteous greeting, his eyes were ringed with dark shadows which told of a night as sleepless as mine, and the table beside him was covered with papers over which he had apparently been brooding.

He at once asked about Aleck.

"He is doing nicely," I replied, sitting down with an exasperated sigh at my own weariness. "As to what caused the attack, it was very like that sudden illness in my rooms on the evening of his twenty-first birthday."

"There is some resemblance," Holmes agreed slowly,

"although I think the differences are greater. In the current incident, we must note the presence of both Mrs. Raleigh and Mr. Moseley."

"I categorically refuse to believe that either of them had anything to do with Aleck's attack," I replied vigorously. "You saw how worried Mr. Moseley appeared—do you mean that that was not genuine?"

"I have not said so."

"And even the faintest suspicion of Winnie is ridiculous. In any case, Holmes," I paused for a moment, for I found this a difficult topic to broach, "there was another person with them at the restaurant: Dan Thatcher."

"Indeed! What is that young man doing in London?"

"You recall that he is not a son of the Thatchers, only a nephew? Since the Thatchers are far from well off and have a growing family of their own to provide for, there is no future for young Thatcher on that small farm."

"So he came to London to look for work?"

"Not exactly." I hesitated again. "He wishes to enter a profession. Winnie insists that this is quite possible, that young Thatcher is both intelligent and surprisingly well educated—apparently, like Aleck, during his village school years he has had some extra lessons from the vicar—and that he is willing to take more coaching, classes, anything in order to advance himself. Winnie also says that . . . that while she was staying at the Roundtrees she encouraged young Thatcher in this course—"

"I was unaware that Mrs. Raleigh knew young Thatcher at that time."

"So was I, and I admit that it surprises me, for ordinarily there is not much intercourse between the gentry of the village and the farm people. However, Winnie says that she and Aleck are going to help young Thatcher on the course he wishes to follow."

"By making inquiries for him here in London?"

"That, certainly, though I also think . . . Winnie was most vehement. 'We haven't much,' she repeated, 'but whatever we have we'll share with Dan.' And he is actually staying with them now, which is why he was included in that luncheon party."

"You appear troubled by all this, doctor."

"It seems . . . strange," I admitted. "And there is more, Holmes. During those long hours in the waiting-room, to pass the time I asked Winnie about her life in America. She chatted away very freely, but . . ."

"Never mentioned that her mother's maiden name was Raleigh?"

"She did not. Of course I am sure that . . . Confound it, Holmes, I hate all this!"

"Let us hope that it is a case of all's well that ends well."

"Surely there is something that you can do, Holmes?"

"Your faith is touching, my dear fellow. What would you suggest?"

"The legacy letter," I urged. "I realise that the copy which Mr. Moseley gave you is inaccurate—"

"So much so that it merits no serious consideration."

"It is still the best copy that we have," I argued, "or are likely to have."

"For the time, yes. Now, doctor, you really should get to bed, for you look completely done in."

"I *am* tired," I agreed with a sigh. "Of course you will not have had time to have any analysis made of that wine?"

"On the contrary," Holmes replied, "I can state positively that there is nothing the matter with the wine in that bottle."

"How can you be so certain?" I asked in surprise.

"Because as soon as I returned here last evening, I had a glass."

"Holmes!"

"There was absolutely no danger, I assure you—will you not try a sample? It is perhaps somewhat lacking in character, but one doesn't expect a particularly robust bouquet from a Beaune."

"Holmes, this is not like you." I was still astonished and also more than a little nettled. "To take such a foolish risk—"

"I repeat, there *was* no risk. By the way, did you notice how particularly thin and drawn Mr. Moseley appeared?"

"He certainly seemed deeply shocked and concerned about Aleck," I agreed.

"I am sure that Mr. Moseley was indeed terribly concerned, but that is not what I meant. I was calling to your attention the fact that he appeared so thin as to be virtually emaciated. You would almost think that he, like Mr. Raleigh of some three years ago, had been enduring genuine starvation. Now, doctor, you really must go to bed."

"I do not move until you have told me what those papers are about," I retorted, for Holmes' long fingers had begun to toy restlessly with the pile on the table before him.

A mischievous gleam lit his tired grey eyes. "Suppose I tell you that they have nothing to do with the case?"

"I shall ask you to give me your word of honour that that is so," I promptly replied.

Holmes gave a comically rueful shake of the head. "I fear that I have had a very bad influence on your character, Watson. When we first met, you would not have dreamed of being so suspicious."

"As in this case my suspicions are quite justified—"

"As they are, I will give you the results of my findings of the past history of Nightsead. You may have noted that when we were making our little visit to that establishment, I was very struck by its appearance?"

"I did," I at once replied, "though what you discovered I cannot guess. I am still sure that my original description of Nightsead, if perhaps brief, was quite accurate."

"As far as it went, yes, but you overlooked the most interesting feature: the relationship of the buildings which remain to the massive heap of rock that lies nearby. Your account left me puzzled as to what could have been the original purpose of the whole gigantic construction, for your thought that it had once formed the dwelling of some mighty baron did not seem likely."

"Why not?"

"The windows, if nothing else. What baronial building of such an age as to have been constructed with stone walls two feet thick and a main hall some seventy feet long would have, on its outer walls too, recessed windows of the height and size of those at Nightsead? Our presumed baron would not only have had to climb a ladder in order to see his enemies approach, he would have had to expose his stalwart person to a fatal arrow from one side whenever he attempted to release a shot to the other. And if there were indeed meant to be no glass in those windows, as of course would have been the case in early medieval times, our baron's lady would, I am sure, have been complaining most bitterly and justly of the winter winds."

I had to admit that, as usual, there was much to be said for Holmes' point of view.

"It is also worth noting," he went on, "that *all* the windows in the two ancient buildings are on the outer walls; this surely suggests that some kind of construction abutted on the opposite blank side and joined the two. Now consider the very revealing placement of that pile of rock, a pile which is obviously part of the original structure that has been torn down. (Not at all an easy task, by the way: the intent for destruction must have been great indeed.)

"The buildings which yet remain can be seen as forming two sides of a rectangle, with that massive heap of rocks forming a third side, parallel to the chief building. Its approximate pattern can even be discerned: its main part ran from west to east, and near the eastern end widened out both north and south.

"Now turn your thoughts to those adjoining chambers used by Mr. Raleigh and his stepfather. Mr. Raleigh's is considerably smaller, yet not only has it a very large entrance door, it has an equally large door which originally communicated with the room next to it, and as well had no hearth: that which is now on the north wall of the room is obviously of quite recent construction. Mr. Moseley's chamber, on the other hand, though it too has an unusually large door, has a wide hearth which has every appearance of being original to the building. And those two chambers have the same kind of windows as the main hall, very high and on the outer walls only."

Here Holmes ceased to speak, and, with a quizzical cock of his head, was obviously waiting for some response from me. Yet, try as I would, I could make nothing of what he had told me.

"Think of that curious little stairway between two windows and near that raised dais," Holmes urged. It was no use. "Is it possible that you still do not see it, Watson? Nightsead was once a monastery."

"A monastery!"

"Certainly: I recognized the probability as soon as I read your most graphic description and had my guess confirmed as soon as I saw the ruins for myself. (Remember that the vicar of the village is very shortsighted; he therefore has never seen the structure as a whole, and neither Mr. Roundtree nor Dr. Leckie has the specialized knowledge which would reveal Nightsead's secret.) The main hall was once the refectory, with the dais in front of that wide hearth reserved for the most important of the fathers; that small staircase led to a pulpit, now broken away, where one of the younger monks would read from some edifying text for the spiritual refreshment of his fellows as they dined. After the meal, the privileged group would leave as they had come, by the door at the end of the dais, and having descended the stone steps into the cloisters—"

"Cloisters!" I exclaimed. "Of course! With a central garden."

"No doubt. Our monks, after a period of quiet exercise, might well move on to gather in the vestry, which is now your friend's chamber, and, shortly thereafter, pass through the common door to attend a meeting in the chapterhouse, presently Mr. Moseley's private room. Then, as the bells called, the good fathers would go on to divine service in the church itself, now reduced to that east-west oriented pile of rock."

As usual with Holmes' explanations, I wondered how I could possibly have missed seeing the right answer myself. "And the high windows?"

"They were designed to let in light while not admitting any sight which might distract the fathers from their labours and devotions."

"The builders of Nightsead?" I asked eagerly. "You have found who they were?"

"Once the original purpose was known, there was no

great difficulty in tracking down at least a short outline of its past. Nightsead was constructed during the twelfth century by an order of the Cistercians, and was a thriving, if small, community at the time when Henry the Eighth first cast eyes on Anne Boleyn."

"Ah!" I exclaimed. "The dissolution of the monasteries."

"Quite so. The monks were summarily evicted, and Nightsead, with all its adjacent lands (then quite considerable), was bestowed on the Earl of Caerles, a lord who was exceedingly adept at 'picking a salad,' as the contemporary phrase so aptly put it, among the properties of others."

"Has the Earl any connection with the Raleigh family?"

Holmes shook his head. "Not as far as I have been able to discover. Yet that in itself is perhaps more encouraging than may at first appear, for Caerles fell out of favour during the minority of Edward the Sixth, and in Mary's reign the property was returned to the Crown. The next record that I could trace belongs to the time of James the First: early in his reign he gave Nightsead, still called the 'monastic lands of St. Bernard,' to his favourite, the Duke of Buckingham."

"The church was not torn down during the dissolution?"

"Oh no, that did not occur until Cromwell's time: his men wrecked the two structures that they found most offensive, the old dormitories and the church. During more recent years, an ancestor of Mr. Raleigh's used some of the fallen rock to build Janet's little cottage, perhaps as a summer home, and no doubt whenever Nightsead was uninhabited (and that must have been a nearly permanent condition), the local people treated the stone as a convenient quarry for their own construction of home and barn, not to mention of those dry-wall fences that snake across the barren hills."

"There is a scattering of small rocks all across the adjacent fields," I agreed, "quite as if they had fallen from wagon or barrow."

"Probably from the dormitories, which were a simple one-storey building and probably made from smaller rocks. Those massive stones of the fallen church have, I think, defeated all pillage."

For a long moment we sat together in silence, and it was I who finally spoke. "Of what are you thinking, Holmes?"

"Of that little carved frog in the Nightsead hall."

"What of it?" I asked in surprise.

"I should like to know when and why it was made. It has been cut in one block of stone, that being used to replace a previous piece, and is of a different composition to those around it. Most certainly that little frog was not part of the original structure of Nightsead."

"Could it not have been?"

Holmes shook his head. "The Cistercian fathers used little ornamentation of any kind. Think of those pillars, as smooth as icicles, as you so aptly wrote, and of the very bosses in the roof, unadorned as soup plates. Can you visualize any religious order which requires construction so plain to permit, much less to command, the creation of that amusing little creature above the Nightsead hearth?"

"Even cathedrals have their oddities, Holmes. The Lincoln imp—"

"Does not look the dean of the chapter right in the eye during every meal."

I admitted the point. "Yet, when all is said and done, Holmes, does the frog matter?"

"All has not been said and done," he replied, "and at the moment I am haunted by the feeling that the final clue is just in front of me and that I am too blind to see it. And the clue, Watson, has the shape of a little stone frog sitting among some very rocky bulrushes."

A few dull days went slowly by. I even returned to the Reading Room, though my scanning of material on Sir Walter Raleigh was desultory at best: I was far more interested in that red-faced man whom *I* at least was sure was the impostor who had tried to obtain a look at Aleck's legacy letter. My hopes were disappointed, however, for I never saw the fellow again.

I finally mentioned this to Holmes.

"I am not surprised," he returned, "for, whoever he was, that precipitous disappearance on the earlier occasion was a little suspicious."

"You think that he was aware that I was trying to follow him and that he was deliberately avoiding me?"

"Possibly. And perhaps avoiding others."

"You mean that he may be known to Aleck and Winnie by sight?"

"That is a possibility," Holmes replied and would say no more.

So matters rested until one morning at breakfast Holmes asked, "Has Mr. Raleigh fully recovered from that attack of illness?"

I nodded.

"Then be so good as to ask him if he could absent himself from his place of employment for an hour this morning. I think the time has come for me to meet your friend."

I did so; Aleck sent the messenger back with his agreement, and he was prompt to his time.

As I had often observed, there was never anyone like Holmes for putting a stranger at ease. In ten minutes he not only had Aleck sitting down in the visitor's chair with every appearance of relaxed comfort, but had told him that he had learned from me of the curious legacy to which my friend was heir and that, being himself a private investigator, he had wondered if he could do anything with the problem.

"I do not see how, Mr. Holmes," Aleck responded. "It is really not the kind of letter which would reveal its secrets to your kind of examination."

"I can but try. If you are willing."

Aleck sat with his slender hands clasped together, his blond head bowed, a thoughtful scowl creasing his brow. So he remained for several moments and then, without moving, said suddenly and abruptly, "It is true that I am being urged by the editor of this new collection of Sir Walter's poems to publish the letter. And it is also true that the terms of the legacy ban nothing except the letter's actual removal from the care of the lawyers. Yet . . . I don't know . . . the letter has been in our family for so long that I feel an absurd repugnance about revealing it, even though I can make little enough of it myself. I have already admitted to Jack," Aleck added with his quick smile, "that I'm a queer fish."

"Perhaps in some ways you are," Holmes returned. "Tell me, Mr. Raleigh, on the evening of your twenty-first birthday when you were so violently ill in Watson's rooms, how much kerosene did you have to swallow to bring on that attack?"

I distinctly heard myself gasp, and then there was total silence for many seconds while Holmes' calmly inquiring eyes remained fixed on Aleck's now raised and hardened face. Then, suddenly throwing up his hands in a comic gesture of defeat, Aleck laughed so heartily that I (though feeling fool enough too) at last joined in.

"You might have warned me, Jack," he said, his eyes still sparkling with amusement. "I never dreamed that you had seen through my little deception that night."

"I didn't," I promptly rejoined. "In fact, I haven't: this is all Holmes' work."

"Then, Mr. Holmes, at least you owe us an explanation," Aleck suggested, still grinning.

"One that you are very welcome to," Holmes replied, leaning back in his chair. "I was perhaps quicker in my deductions because I have myself produced the very symptoms from which you were suffering when Watson first saw you on his return—weakness, pallor, loss of weight—by simple starvation. Since you had been attended only by an elderly physician of no great learning, since for some time your condition remained the same with no more evident signs of illness appearing, and since you could even at that time force yourself to continue the studies in which you were so passionately interested, I began to wonder if your symptoms were not more in your control than old Dr. Abernathy guessed. Especially since you had a very good reason for your actions: you wished to convince Mr. Moseley that you should remain in London."

"Quite right," Aleck rejoined. "And of course my plan failed, for my apparent decline only gave my stepfather the opportunity to point out how much healthier I had been in the country. So I determined to make a last effort by making myself very demonstrably sick, with Doctor Jack as the witness. I knew that I had little chance of changing my stepfather's mind, but I was really desperate enough to try anything."

"No wonder you ate heartily at your birthday supper," I exclaimed. "You must have been famished."

"I think Mr. Raleigh's appetite was caused more by his decision to make himself convincingly ill by swallowing kerosene," Holmes commented drily.

Aleck, laughing once more, agreed. "Only kerosene is such beastly stuff that I knew that both I and the chamber would reek of it, so I had decided to knock your lamp to the floor, Jack. But I had no sooner forced down a mouthful than I became so terribly sick that I promptly dropped the lamp. I was afraid that you would notice the way the broken pieces had fallen—"

"I noticed," I interrupted, somewhat sourly, "but thought nothing of it. I suppose," turning to Holmes, "you guessed the true cause of Aleck's sudden sickness from that broken lamp?"

"Partly, yes," he replied, "for I could not see why knocking a lamp to the floor during the paroxysms of sickness should also unscrew the burner. How about your recent sudden illness in the restaurant, Mr. Raleigh? Have you any explanation for that?"

"None," Aleck replied, adding with a grin, "unless it is divine punishment for my earlier deception."

"How much of your glass of wine had you drunk, Mr. Raleigh?"

"I really don't remember," Aleck answered frankly. "I was too full of my latest discovery to pay much attention to anything else."

"Your latest discovery?"

"That the maiden name of Sir Walter's mother was Champernowne, the same as that of the firm of lawyers which has the perpetual keeping of the Raleigh letter. I know that this doesn't sound like much, but it is really the first substantial connection I have found between Sir Walter and that letter, and thus it is important to me— very."

Holmes agreed and asked, "Are you aware that Nightsead was once a Cistercian monastery, Mr. Raleigh?"

Aleck's stunned expression was sufficient denial, and Holmes quickly outlined his findings.

"Remarkable," Aleck commented. "I'm afraid that I have as yet paid little attention to the history of Nightsead; as far as my research into Raleigh himself has gone, I have found no connection. I congratulate you, Mr. Holmes: that was good work."

"Then you will consider my proposition concerning your legacy, Mr. Raleigh?"

Aleck hesitated. "If I accept any help, Mr. Holmes," he said finally, "it shall be yours." With that, and a quick smile, he left.

One evening later that week we heard the quick tread of a man on the street below. Holmes put down his notebook, I lowered my paper: yes, the steps had turned in at our Baker Street door.

It was Aleck.

"My research is revealing much that is interesting about Sir Walter Raleigh," he began in his abrupt way, "but nothing about my legacy. So I have decided that either you solve the mystery, Mr. Holmes, or I allow the letter to be published in the Raleigh biography and at least earn a few extra shillings from it that way."

"What has changed your mind, Mr. Raleigh?"

"Two discoveries. One," he said with a shy smile, "that Winnie is, as Dickens would say, in an interesting condition."

Of course we congratulated him.

"No doubt you will have much use for any extra money that the biography can earn," I added.

"No doubt we will, Jack, but it isn't just that. You see, one reason that, once I had seen my legacy letter, I never took it too seriously was that Sir Walter Raleigh wasn't known to have had great riches. Oh, he had some nice monopolies in trade, and some estates which were pretty good too, and he did well enough now and then out of some of his sea activities (piracy, really), but he never seemed to have been truly wealthy. And of course he was such a flamboyant chap that his expenses must have been enormous."

"And your second discovery concerns treasure of some sort?" I asked eagerly. "Sir Walter *did* find a 'great treasure'?"

"He found it all right," Aleck replied, grinning, "the question is how much he was able to keep. You see, Raleigh had been the leader of an expedition aimed at capturing one of the Spanish treasure fleets on its way home from South America—that's what Drake had done, and the queen had not only knighted him for it, she had kept both government and court afloat for years on just her share of the booty. The expedition that Raleigh had planned was even luckier: it intercepted a Portuguese carrack from the East Indies, laden with spices, ebony, ivory, jewels, silver, gold—contemporaries believed it the richest prize ever taken by the British."

"Then certainly Sir Walter would have become a very wealthy man!" I exclaimed.

"He would have, Jack, except that he was not with

his ships. The queen had clapped him in the Tower for privately marrying Bess Throckmorton, one of her maids of honour."

"Why should they not have married?" I asked, surprised.

"People near in service to the queen formed a pretty closed circle, Jack, and marriages among them were invariably part of the power manoeuvring of the time; hence the queen's approval was a political (though not a legal) necessity. For two who lived in the intense limelight that surrounded the queen secretly to court and marry for love was a most dangerous precedent to that society, and Elizabeth's reaction was accordingly tempestuous."

"So Sir Walter missed the biggest chance of his life, and missed it for love," I sighed.

"The love is unquestioned, for it lasted all Raleigh's life, but he only partially missed his chance at a haul of treasure. He was quickly released from the Tower because no one else could control the immense looting of the ship that started as soon as the vessel docked—common sailors were said to have so stuffed their pockets that they were giving lumps of pure amber for a tankard of ale. The queen had helped finance the expedition and was frantic to have her full share of the haul."

"And did she get it?" I asked.

"Ah, that's the question. The queen complained vigorously that she did not . . . but of course that's precisely what one would expect her to say. Sir Walter, on the other hand, always claimed equally vigorously that *he* was the injured party and that he was barely able to cover expenses, which, again, is what one would expect *him* to say. What *is* very clear is that Raleigh knew that he had deeply offended the queen and might never again be permitted to have a chance of a good haul of booty. So if he had come across something in that ship's hold which was small and yet immensely valuable . . ."

"You think that your ancestor would have pocketed it?"

"I am quite sure that he would, without hesitation, taking it as only his due. And by all accounts the loot from that Portuguese ship was spectacular."

"Which brings us . . . where?" Holmes had been watching Aleck keenly.

"Here," Aleck replied simply, pulling out of his pocket a folded sheet of paper. "I've spent a couple of hours at the lawyers this afternoon, my memory is pretty fair, and I've tried to write clearly."

"A copy of the Raleigh letter?" Holmes jerked upright in his chair.

"A copy of the Raleigh letter," Aleck agreed. "If you could deduce my kerosene trick from Jack's account of my birthday supper, Mr. Holmes, perhaps you'll be able to make something of this." He spread the paper open on the table between us.

*A laast bless you. You knoe whaat hevvi Chaarge
I have agaaist the Faather, that the Sunne hath
done whaat Hee hath wee must be Thaankfull.
Pooar roial fuule Hee is like enoff to soffer as mi
dere mort Loord whoos leps I yet kess. Therefoor*

*keep the Doobel Haart hoole and whaar hit is I
praie you and at the laast let mi grate Treshur bee
there also, foor you ded ever hold your Sole in your
owne Teeth and Hee was ever with God whaatever
thei ded sai. I do moche thenk of when wee were
Cheldren and to proove hit doo sine miself as we ded
then.*

To dere *from his dere*

I had always felt that if Holmes could only see a
true copy of the Raleigh letter, the solution of the legacy
mystery would be at hand. I could no longer think so,
for this copy, though considerably different, was fully
as inexplicable as that which Mr. Moseley had left with
Holmes.

As well, all the major questions remained. Who was
the father, against whom the writer had a "hevvi
Chaarge," who the son, the "pooar roial fuule"? Who
was the "dere mort Loord," and how, if "mort" indeed
meant "dead," could the writer yet kiss his lips? What
was the "Doobel Haart" which was to be kept whole,
and (most important of all) where had it been put?
Wherever that was, the recipient of the letter had been
instructed to put the writer's "grate Treshur" also. As
for those scribbles at the bottom of the letter, I could
only clutch my head in frustration.

For some moments Holmes and I stared at the sheet
of paper.

"Can you make anything of it, Holmes?" I finally
asked.

He shook his head thoughtfully. "Not at the moment, no. What is your opinion of the letter, Mr. Raleigh?"

"The handwriting of the original is certainly not that of Sir Walter, nor yet of the queen. In fact, it is rather sprawling and irregular, not that of an educated Elizabethan at all. As for those drawings at the end, they are just as sloppy a scrawl as I've made them: I would guess that they are symbols which the writer and recipient had used to each other for so long that the merest indication of them was enough for understanding. The Elizabethans *did* love word play of all kinds, you know. Leicester had heavy eyes, and Elizabeth nicknamed him 'Lids'; thereafter he would sign notes to her with a drawn eye."

"Did Sir Walter have a court nickname?" I asked.

"Oh yes, the obvious pun on his Christian name, 'Water.' There were silly jokes about the queen's being thirsty for 'Water,' and, after Raleigh fell from favour, that 'Water' was damned indeed—that kind of thing. But I can't see any way that either of those two scribbles at the bottom of my letter can be meant to convey the meaning of water, and in any case the nicknames were apparently from childhood."

"The letter's opening—that 'laast bless you'—sounds as if the message was sent late in the writer's life," Holmes mused, "not that that takes us any farther at the moment. Do you have any thoughts on the identity of the father and son, Mr. Raleigh? Since the son is royal, presumably the father is also."

"The most obvious pair would be Leicester and Essex,

although Essex was really only a son by marriage and his royal blood was pretty well diluted. There's another point, though: 'to suffer' was an Elizabethan euphemism for 'executed,' and that would fit Essex very well: he had led a monumentally stupid rebellion—very much a royal fool."

"What does 'mort' mean, Aleck?" I asked.

"I can make nothing of it, Jack, unless it means either 'dying' or—an interesting possibility—'condemned to death,' in which case of course it could refer to Essex. Really, there is so much that is inexplicable in my legacy letter that the only hopeful note I can find is that it does mention treasure. 'Grate Treshur' at that."

"Can you not make something of it, Holmes?" I again urged.

But he had turned to Aleck. "Have you shown this copy to anyone else, Mr. Raleigh?"

"No. I came right here from the lawyers."

"Have you ever made a copy before?"

"No. I have paraphrased the letter, verbally, for Winnie. That's all."

"When?"

"On numerous occasions," Aleck returned, looking surprised. "In fact, Winnie has kept urging me to make a good copy of the letter, but, after I had seen it, I never again really took it too seriously—it didn't seem possible that such a muddle could, after all these years, lead to anything. What do you think, Mr. Holmes?"

"Little enough as yet," he replied, "and yet enough that I would like to ask you to keep your making of the copy a secret for the time being. *Even from Mrs. Raleigh.*"

Aleck paused, then nodded. "Very well, Mr. Holmes: for the time being the secret shall remain with you and Jack." With that, and the promise to look in again in a few days, he left.

"Apparently Mrs. Raleigh's interest in the legacy remains keen," Holmes then remarked.

"Why should it not?" I demanded.

Holmes made no reply, only remained slumped in his chair while the smoke from his pipe gathered around him. Then he abruptly rose and, unlocking the drawer of his desk devoted to the Raleigh case, tossed the letter in.

"The ancient Israelites complained of having to make brick without straw," he commented wryly. "I am in the even more difficult position of trying to make bricks without clay. All this," flipping his fingers through the contents of the drawer, "is straw, nothing but straw. We know so much, even to the true wording of the Raleigh letter, and yet nothing holds together. Although there is something about that letter . . . 'laast,' 'pooar,' 'doobel,' 'proove' . . . ." He paused, staring into space.

I waited, and waited in vain. "What do you propose to do?" I finally asked.

Holmes slammed the drawer shut and locked it. "I have no choice: continue to collect straw. And hope that I can still recognize a lump of clay if I should be so fortunate as to find one."

* * *

But it was I who gathered the next handful of straw (to continue Holmes' metaphor).

Several days had gone by when at breakfast one morning Holmes suddenly asked, "You haven't yet decided on a practice, have you, Watson?"

"You know very well that I haven't. Why else am I perusing those confounded advertisements in the medical journals?" I passed Holmes the marmalade. "What do you want me to do?"

"Would it not be natural if you were to ask the advice of Dr. Leckie as to what country practices are available?"

"In other words, you wish me to go to the village."

"I would like to know more about Janet and more about the Thatcher family," Holmes admitted. "I would go myself except that I have a certain reluctance about intruding myself so directly on the area's notice at this time. You, on the other hand, are quite well enough known there to be taken for granted, and your seeing Dr. Leckie should arouse no special interest. You could go today?"

"I could."

"Then I will wish you, not a pleasant journey (which, I fear, is impossible), but a successful one. Write me at once, if you'll be so good, and wire if there is anything at all surprising."

At the village I went at once to the little public house and, after supper, called on Dr. Leckie. As I expected, his evening surgery was very quiet, and he was delighted

to see me. I sent my first letter to Holmes before I retired for the night.

My dear Holmes,

Little news so far. During our first conversation
Dr. Leckie did confirm what Aleck had told me, that
his mother died of typhoid, complicated by the ad-
vanced stages of her pregnancy. She had apparently thought that her illness was due only to her
condition and accordingly did not have Dr. Leckie
summoned until it was far too late for him to do
anything—indeed, she died shortly after he reached
Nightsead.

Dr. Leckie has invited me to go over his books to
gain some idea of the operating costs of a rural
practice. If it were not that I must in truth consider
such a purchase before long, I would feel guilty for
my deceit. As it is, I shall make good use of my time.

Yours,

Watson

Holmes' reply was immediate and typical.

My dear Watson,

Your feelings of guilt seem to be easily aroused.
I trust that they are as easily laid to rest.

All that is new here is that I have heard from a
correspondent in America. There is no doubt: Mrs.
Raleigh's mother was far more conversant with her
family history than were your friend's people, and
Mrs. Raleigh is not only a proven descendant of

Sir Walter, the young lady knew this *before she left for England*.

Yours,
Holmes

I wrote again the next day, although I could not bring myself to comment on the revelation concerning Winnie, for I had total faith in her innocence and constancy no matter what the evidence.

My dear Holmes,

I would like to know what would trouble *your* conscience. Or perhaps I would rather not know.

Dr. Leckie has told me a few details about Janet. She left a brutal husband in Scotland and had recently started working on the Thatchers' farm when Mr. Moseley moved his family to Nightstead and was looking for a servant. I said that I thought that Janet could have done much better for herself in some other area, and Dr. Leckie replied, "Janet is a good woman, and I think fond of Aleck. Also, she likes her own way, and at Nightstead she has had it." No doubt this is all true.

I shall look into the Thatchers tomorrow.

Yours,
Watson

But I then came across a sight which, later that same day, made me write again.

Holmes,

This will be a blunt letter, for in truth I am in no mood to write otherwise.

Late this afternoon I took a walk from the village up the Nightsead hill, planning to use the outing as an excuse to call at the Thatcher farmhouse for a glass of milk. As I approached the lower field, movement in a clump of bushes to my right caught my attention, and I stopped. Holmes, I assure you that I am not mistaken: it was Janet and that young man in moleskin. More, *they were in the act of dalliance*, she leaning her head on his shoulder as they slowly walked along.

I find this as outrageous as will you, for the man is obviously young—I would say younger than Aleck.

There is obviously more to Janet's remaining at Nightsead than we thought.

Watson

Holmes' reply was prompt, if calm.

My dear Watson,

I have long thought that Janet had very good reason for remaining so faithfully at Nightsead. As for the relative ages of the two, Janet cannot be more years older than the young man than your friend's mother was when she married Ivor Moseley. On such a subject, what man is brave enough to call himself an expert?

As for me, I am still looking for clay.

Yours,

Holmes

My next discovery was such that I returned the following day and announced it as soon as I entered our sitting-room. "Holmes, Janet's young swain is Dan Thatcher!"

"You are quite sure?"

"Positive. More, Dan Thatcher is not only red-headed and a big young fellow, he is full-faced, of a florid complexion, and, I am convinced, has the same way of striding along as that impostor in the Museum!"

"You saw him yourself?" Holmes was watching me keenly. "At close range?"

"I did. He came into the inn for a glass of beer, and I watched him for the better part of an hour."

"Not too obtrusively, I hope?" Holmes murmured. "All right, Watson, all right—I see from the glint in your eye that you have more news for me."

"I do. *Dan Thatcher is the only red-headed man in that area.* After he left, I commented to the innkeeper about the fellow's hair. He agreed that it was an uncommon colour and added that there were no other redheads anywhere near, Thatcher's complexion being accounted for by his being a 'foreigner'—he is the Thatchers' nephew, not their son, you remember, and comes from somewhere up north. More, unlike some countrymen, he has apparently no objection to making a trip to London: his staying with Winnie and Aleck proves that."

I paused, expecting some comment from Holmes, for I felt that my identification of Dan Thatcher as the red-headed man at the Museum and therefore most probably as the impostor on Aleck's birthday was a giant step forward. "Young Thatcher does not at the moment have either beard or moustache," I finally went on, "but no doubt they were assumed for the time in order to make him look older, for he is of course younger than Aleck." When Holmes still remained silent, I added my last item of information, insignificant though it seemed to me. "There is another oddity about the fellow: his name is truly Dan, not Daniel."

Holmes suddenly straightened. "You are sure of that, doctor?"

I nodded. "It apparently is quite a joke in the area that from the smallest boy Dan Thatcher would insist that he never be called Daniel because it was not his name."

Holmes had reached down his old Bible and was thumbing the concordance at the back. Expecting some revelation, I sat on patiently, only to have Holmes thrust the volume back onto the shelf and exclaim, impatiently, "More straw, Watson, nothing but more straw."

And getting up, he took himself off to bed.

This was the time of that peculiar autumn fog which descended on London that year, yellow, oily, clammy and suffocating. My spirits had been worsened by my still not having found a medical practice at once fitted to my interests and my pocketbook; I had sent out yet another batch of inquiries and, while waiting for replies, was frequently reduced to taking long evening strolls to relieve my boredom.

Holmes too seemed both restless and strangely uncommunicative, and so I was most surprised when, as I was taking up my hat and stick, he proposed joining me.

"If I shall not intrude," he added with his customary courtesy.

"Far from it," I assured him honestly. "My own company has little appeal at the end of a long day."

"Then let us go in search of a good appetite for dinner," Holmes rejoined, and so we set out.

Neither of us had any other purpose in our walk, and it was pure chance that took us, a little over an hour later, to the street leading to the lodging-house where Aleck and Winnie resided.

Holmes paused to stare along the way. "Would you be so good as to show the house to me?"

"Certainly," I replied, "if you will be so good as to tell me why you wish to see the house rather than its inhabitants."

"Because," Holmes replied drily, "if we make this little detour, we shall return home promptly for dinner."

Laughingly agreeing that this was as good a reason as any we had had for our activities that evening, I led the way. As we neared the modest brick structure, the door flew open and a stout little woman in a flowered wrapper popped out.

"It *is* Dr. Watson, ain't it?" She peered down at

me from the steps. "You wouldn't 'ave seen Mrs. Raleigh, would you, sir? Nor yet Mr. Raleigh?" I of course shook my head. "And their supper aruinin' of itself on the 'ob this very minute! Mrs. Raleigh went h'out ages ago, 'eadin' for that there Readin' Room, which I don't think is a 'ealthy place for a young 'ooman in 'er condition. 'You'll be back prompt for supper, now won't you?' I says, 'for you knows 'ow Mr. Raleigh does fret if 'e thinks you're over tirin' of yourself.' 'I won't be late,' she says, but then she allus says so, and like as not comes 'ome fair runnin' with 'er 'at 'angin' by its strings. But tonight she ain't come yet, and Mr. Raleigh, 'e got that full of the fidgets awaitin' for 'er that nothin' will do but 'e must go after 'er, and now 'e ain't back neither, and their supper'll be worse than nothin' by the time they gets to it, for a shepherd's pie won't sit quiet all this time, no matter where you puts it—"

Here I broached the torrent of words to say that we would follow Aleck and Winnie's path as it was on our own route back and would, if we should see them, advance the claim of the neglected shepherd's pie.

We set off at a brisk pace, watching both sides of the way and pausing at each intersection to examine our fellow pedestrians, but we reached the steps of the British Museum without seeing a sign of my friends.

"They have gone another way," I suggested.

"Strange, since they are late and we came by the shortest path," Holmes returned thoughtfully. "Do you know, Watson, I don't quite like this."

"Surely there is no harm that could have come to

them?" I asked, surprised. "It is not yet more than dusk, the fog is quite light, and . . . to *both* of them?"

"Not to both, no. And there is a place where it is always dusk." He set off again, back the way we had come, and I quickly followed. "If Mrs. Raleigh were late in leaving the Reading Room and wished to cut off some of the length of her journey, there is an alley which she might take." He paused.

Across from us was the entrance to what appeared to be little more than a tunnel between two high buildings.

"Surely Winnie would not enter that," I protested, for with the fog beginning to settle in the night chill, that alley looked a noisome hole indeed.

"Mrs. Raleigh does not sound like a timid woman," Holmes rejoined, and I had to agree that he was right in his assessment.

We crossed the street and plunged into that alley. At once I stumbled, for broken cobbles were under my feet, and the brick walls, dripping with the sooty grime of the years, were so close that they nearly brushed our shoulders. Here the fog had not so much entered as cut off what fading light there had been in the road outside, shut in, too, the myriad unpleasant aromas that mankind leaves in such a place. There was also a curious deadness to the air so that all sounds seemed swallowed up; the bustle of the busy thoroughfare that we had just left did not penetrate here, and even the regular fall of our boots rose up to our ears dull and distant.

I quickly lost sense of both direction and distance. We were angling off to the left, I could tell, as the enclosing buildings, tall as canyon walls, wove their ancient way from one London area to another, and I think that we had covered perhaps a hundred yards when the alley both widened and, with a brief jog around a jutting corner, turned sharp right. We travelled on only a short distance—perhaps fifty feet—when Holmes abruptly and briefly stopped. I, who had been at his heels, now stepped beside him, and what I saw ahead halted me also.

A bundle of rags had been flung against the base of the left wall, only the bundle had long dark hair cascading onto the dirt of those broken cobbles, and I knew that it was Winnie—her little brown hat lay crushed by one outflung hand. A man, tall and in a dark overcoat, leaned over her, and as he looked up I saw that it was Aleck.

Or, rather, what had been Aleck: this man I recognized by his clothing, his build, his colouring—by the common sense that told me that it was indeed he. But his light eyes stared blankly at me, his thin face was twisted into rigid lines, and he was breathing in strangled gasps.

All this took only a second. Then Holmes sprang forward, and I followed. As Holmes grasped Aleck, pulling him upright, I dropped beside Winnie, and my first glance automatically registered both relief and fear: she was alive, for the blood that was trickling down her neck was still flowing; she was frighteningly near death, for I could see no perceptible breathing.

I heard Holmes' firm voice—"Stand still, Mr. Raleigh"—and then his rapid footsteps retreating down the alley. In moments he was back and, pausing only to mutter to me, "I've sent for the police," as rapidly disappeared on down the alley. Again he was quickly back, too quickly I knew to have found any sign of Winnie's attacker.

All this time Aleck had remained leaning against the wall, gasping hoarsely and gazing down at Winnie with wide, staring eyes that, as I could tell, saw nothing. He kept convulsively opening and shutting his hands, as if they troubled him, and I saw that they were streaked with blood.

"What happened, Mr. Raleigh?" Holmes asked in a calm, clear voice.

In jerky fragments Aleck told of his going to meet Winnie, of his not finding her, of his then retracing his steps and pausing by the alley, and finally of his entering it.

"Once," he ran on, "when we were together and late, Winnie led me here. I told her . . . never, never go this way alone . . . She laughed . . . 'Promise,' I said, 'promise you won't . . .' She laughed . . . just laughed . . ."

"When did you find her, Mr. Raleigh?"

"When? What do you mean. . . ? Now, right now. I turned down the alley, and kept on and on, I was nearly running, I nearly ran into her, I couldn't stop, I couldn't—"

"Aleck," I looked up and spoke very sternly, "*stop that*. Pull yourself together."

Then he was quiet, save for his sobbing breath, and that seemed to shake the alley.

"How is she, doctor?" Holmes leaned over me to ask.

I glanced at Aleck, but he appeared near comatose, sagging low against the wall, eyes now closed. "It's bad, Holmes," I answered in a whisper. "It's very bad."

"Hit on the back of the head?" I nodded. "Skull fractured?"

"I think not. Concussion and shock, bad shock."

"She has been here for some time, then?"

"It's impossible to say for sure, of course, but I would not expect such deep trauma to follow immediately on the blow. Ah," I exclaimed with relief, "here come the police."

"And for once," Holmes stood up, "I am glad to see them."

It was early morning before we met again at our Baker Street rooms, for I had stayed at the hospital until I was satisfied that the dark angel had ceased to hover over Winnie's slight form.

Holmes looked up as soon as I entered, and I answered the question in his sleepless eyes.

"Unless matters unexpectedly worsen, she will live. Will, I think, recover fully."

"And her child?"

"It is too early to say. She is not haemorrhaging, however, and that is good."

"Then come, my dear fellow," Holmes was lifting a

cover off a small platter on the table, "Mrs. Hudson has kindly left us some sandwiches."

"I hardly feel hungry, Holmes."

"What would you prescribe for anyone else in your state of exhaustion? Quite so. Then come, doctor, try your own medicine, and let me fill your glass."

Holmes was, of course, quite right, and my appetite returned as I ate.

"Did you discover anything in that alley, Holmes?"

He shook his head. "Mrs. Raleigh's attacker was not considerate enough to drop a button from his coat or throw away a half-smoked cigar. And though those cobbles were filthy, they held nothing of interest. The police have not found Mrs. Raleigh's pocket-book?" For this had been missing.

"Not as far as I know."

"Nor, I think, will they."

"It isn't much loss, for Aleck is sure that Winnie would have had only a few shillings with her."

"Nor was the pocket-book itself of much value. Mrs. Andrews tells me—"

"You have been back to their lodging-house?" I asked, surprised.

"I thought that someone ought to notify the good lady as to what had happened."

"In other words, you wanted to ask Mrs. Andrews about Winnie's pocket-book."

"I did, yes, for I thought the landlady would have a better eye for such things than the husband. The pocket-book, Mrs. Andrews says, was 'a bit of a leather thing near threadbare'; if inaccurate, the description is telling enough. And Mrs. Raleigh, I noted, was quite shabbily dressed: not an obvious mark for a thief."

"Surely thieves are not always selective, Holmes. Whatever Winnie had would be well worth stealing to someone."

"Quite true, yet there are some problems with the theory that a random villain was responsible for the attack on Mrs. Raleigh. Where, for instance, did he come from?"

I could see no problem. "He came off the street, as we did."

"Then why did he not attack Mrs. Raleigh long before he did? The longer he waited, the longer he crept along behind her, the more likely was it that someone else would enter the alley, or that Mrs. Raleigh would become aware of his presence and scream so loudly that she would be heard on the street. And should rescuers enter from both ends, the would-be thief would have been trapped with no escape possible."

"Perhaps he came from the other way," I suggested, "from the direction that Winnie was going towards, and merely happened to meet her."

"From where she was felled to the far end, the alley runs straight. Mrs. Raleigh would therefore have been able to see her attacker approaching and surely would have turned and fled: she would not continue to advance towards a rough-appearing stranger."

"I should not think so," I conceded. "Winnie has much courage, but she is certainly not foolhardy."

"There is also the fact that the alley *is* very narrow, and Mrs. Raleigh, hit at the nape of the neck, fell forward. The supposition is therefore strong that the attack came from behind her."

"There is that jog in the alley," I recalled, "just before the spot where Winnie lay. If a man were lurking there . . ."

"Again that would mean a chance attack."

"Is that not most likely, Holmes?"

"There are a few points which disturb me. This chance attacker has something with him heavy enough to knock Mrs. Raleigh senseless in one blow."

"A professional burglar would have a jemmy or something like it in his pocket, would he not?"

"He might, although he would be asking for trouble to be lurking in that alley during early evening hours with such a weapon in his possession: the bobbies regularly patrol it. Also, suppose a professional thief, with such a professional weapon as you describe, was indeed lurking in that jog in the alley, spied Mrs. Raleigh as an approaching victim, albeit not a very well-dressed one, and attacked her. Why would he not take her wedding ring? It is quite a good one, I noticed. Or the fine gold chain that she had about her neck?"

"He was alarmed by something before he could do so," I suggested.

"By what? Remember how isolated that stretch of

the alley is, and remember that we are considering a professional thief, hardly the fellow to jump at the meow of a stray cat. There is another point that bothers me, Watson: Mrs. Raleigh's hat."

"It was totally crushed by the force of the blow."

"Exactly. It was a small bit of millinery, styled to sit on the back of the head like a helmet."

"It did fit so," I agreed, surprised, for though I had often seen Winnie wear it, Holmes had seen only the broken fragments lying on the alley's cobbles.

"Also it was made of a dark brown material that appeared to be a heavy felt while in reality being no more than a sort of flannel. Yet this chance attacker, this professional thief, lying in wait while Mrs. Raleigh approaches him, with her temples bare of both hat and hair, chooses to strike at the nape of the neck, apparently confident that that solid-appearing little hat is nothing more than a wisp of soft yardage."

"You would expect him to have hit at the side of the head?"

"I would, yes. A professional could give a tap there that would down a woman in a trice and yet leave her undamaged, and a professional usually has a very healthy respect for his own skin. It is almost as if Mrs. Raleigh's attacker saw her leave the Museum, knew her habits well enough to realize that, late as she was, she would take the alley shortcut, hurried to lie in wait for her, struck her down so viciously that he could well have killed her, and then grabbed her pocket-book to give an ostensible explanation for the attack. And now, doctor, what is troubling you? For ever since you returned your face has made it clear that something is."

I had not intended telling anything to Holmes, yet now I could not hold it back, for I was indeed deeply distressed. "While I was sitting at Winnie's side, Holmes, and Aleck was still being interviewed by the police, she suddenly roused and with a wild and frightened look, said, 'I should have told him. I should have told him.'"

"That was all?"

"That was all. Said it repeatedly until she again lost consciousness. 'I should have told him.'"

"Yet there is, I think, something more on your mind, doctor?"

"Aleck told me that, in trying to trace the genealogy of his branch of the Raleigh family, he had just come across documents that strongly suggest that Winnie's own family is closely connected to his. He had been prepared to run home delighted with the surprise that he thought that he had for Winnie when he discovered, by a chance remark of an attendant, that Winnie had been researching in those very documents herself."

"So even if she had previously been ignorant of the possible connection, of her possible claim on the Raleigh legacy, she knew then."

"Precisely. Aleck was so shocked at her silence that he dropped his own work and concentrated on Winnie's background. He quickly realized that she is *next in line to the Raleigh legacy*."

"He did not tell her of his discovery?"

I shook my head. "He felt that it would be no news to her."

"And his reaction to this?"

I hesitated. "He is stunned. Stunned to a degree I would not have expected."

"I think that when a man has built his life's happiness on the foundation of another's truthfulness, seeing that foundation quiver must be a shock next to madness," Holmes rejoined quietly.

"I agree, although I am sure—*sure*, Holmes—that Winnie is innocent of all wrongdoing."

"I have not said otherwise, doctor. I am only viewing her behaviour as it must have suddenly appeared to Mr. Raleigh. He told you all this at the hospital, did he?"

"He did, although 'told' is much too lucid a description for the broken fragments of speech that came, at long intervals, from Aleck's lips. And there was a policeman leaning against the wall, taking notes, all the time."

"Naturally. Did Mr. Raleigh pay him any attention?"

"None. I am sure Aleck was unaware of his presence. Holmes . . ." I paused and tried again. "There *is* a case which could be made against Aleck, isn't there? The police *could* wonder if he were himself Winnie's attacker?"

"A case could be made, certainly." Holmes rose and, going to the window, flung it wide. "Dawn," he murmured, looking out, "and a new day. What will it bring, I wonder?" Leaning against the sash, he turned to me.

"Mr. Raleigh knew that, when Mrs. Raleigh was late leaving the Reading Room, she would take that alley shortcut, and she was late last night. He had very recently made a discovery that had left him feeling betrayed by his wife. The alley is long, narrow, dim, sound deadening, and highly unlikely to be inhabited: in other words, an excellent place for him to make the attack. Even the fog would have helped, for its drifting nature meant that no one was apt to observe a solitary man slipping into that opening. And, in fact, as far as I could ascertain, no one *did* notice. As well, Mr. Raleigh would naturally know that his wife's little hat was far too flimsy to be of any protection to her from a blow."

"What did he use for a weapon?" I demanded.

"Excellent, Watson." Holmes gave a nod of approval. "Mr. Raleigh had nothing on him that would have served that purpose, for I made a rough search of his clothing while I assisted him to stand up. Nor was there anything left in or near the alley. That, however, is negative evidence of a very weak kind, for he could well have secreted a brick in his pocket and flung it into a passing dray afterwards, only then returning to stand by his wife, waiting for them to be found. In that case, the state of shock in which we found him could have been caused by bitter guilt as much as by grief. Oh yes, a case could be made against him."

"But you are not prepared to make that case?" I urged, hoping desperately that my supposition was correct.

Holmes turned and closed the window. "Dan Thatcher is again staying with Mr. and Mrs. Raleigh. Or so Mrs. Andrews says; he was out when I called, in fact had been out most of the afternoon."

I digested this for a moment. "Why should he harm Winnie?"

"Why should anyone, except Mr. Raleigh and that only during an insane moment of fury? I think a nap will enable me to face the day better, doctor, so, as the lightening sky forbids a good night, I will say good morning."

I too retired to my room, but I could not sleep.

The next few days were horribly long for me. The good news of Winnie's steady recovery and of there being no sign of a miscarriage was much diluted by the all too great evidence of a strain between her and Aleck. They said little, but they had begun to watch each other, sending covert glances while ostensibly speaking to me, quick looks of pain, of bewilderment, of loss which have no place between a loving man and wife. I would gladly have stayed away from the hospital altogether, but both Winnie and Aleck were all too eager to have me present, so I dragged myself there day after day, and I hardly know which of the three of us was the most miserable.

Nor was Aleck's research into the biography and works of Sir Walter Raleigh any longer a subject in which we could happily lose ourselves: he had totally ceased going to the Reading Room, had stopped working on the rough draft that he had already completed, and was surly and uncommunicative even with me. Winnie was at last released from hospital, wan and thin, but the gloom over her and Aleck only deepened with every passing day.

For some time I had kept my own counsel; finally I told Holmes all, ending with the heartfelt exclamation, "Will nothing break this accursed legacy case!"

"I am hoping so," he replied. "In fact, I rather think I shall take a little trip into Devonshire."

"Devonshire!" I stared at him in utter astonishment. "For pity's sake, Holmes, why?"

"Lovely countryside, I understand."

"Much you care about lovely countryside," I retorted, for my companion's total indifference to even the most awesome sights of Nature had often been a bone of contention between us. "What has got into you, Holmes?"

"I must admit that I am worried by this attack on Mrs. Raleigh. I have a heavy foreboding that there is more violence ahead, and, while I can sense and fear it, I am helpless to prevent its occurrence."

"You do not yet suspect anyone?" I asked.

"Oh, 'suspect'!" Holmes waved that aside with one impatient hand. "Leave suspicion and all like emotions to the writers of romances. I deal with facts, and that is part of my present problem. We know so much, and yet still nothing hangs together." He stretched out his long legs to the fire. "We know that some twenty years ago Mr. Raleigh's mother married Ivor Moseley at Baccarat—"

"Which is a glass-refining centre," I interjected, "or so you said."

"Quite so. Mr. Raleigh's mother, no longer a young woman, was soon pregnant and ill and wanted to return to England; as the only property either she or her husband then had was Nightsead, the little family moved there. Soon Mr. Raleigh's mother died, but her husband and son remained."

"No doubt from lack of funds," I suggested.

"No doubt. Yet through the years Mr. Moseley has managed to finance occasional trips to London. He also walks regularly into the village in order to read Mr. Roundtree's copies of *The Times*."

"Reading *The Times* is hardly a strange occupation for a gentleman, Holmes."

"I did not say that it was; I merely point out that it is—and for years has been—an occupation of Mr. Moseley's. He allows his young stepson to think that he is his natural father, and, though keeping his own room door locked, apparently to keep the young lad out, later gives him all the books of poetry that he has in his own small library, a library devoted to the Elizabethans and a collection of books from which all the flyleaves have been removed.

"During all those early years Janet remains in her cottage, caring for the needs of her master and his young stepson and visiting the Thatchers, poor neighbouring farmers who are yet rearing a nephew, a boy who is red-headed, is said to have come from 'up north,' is several years younger than Mr. Raleigh, and always insists that his name is Dan, not Daniel. Considering the comparative proximity of the two homes and the fact that both boys were taking lessons from the village vicar, one would have expected that the two lads would have become friends, but they did not: Janet prevented it."

"Is this of any importance to the matter of the legacy, Holmes?"

"Who can say, doctor? I am merely reciting such facts as we have. So matters go until Mr. Raleigh, having finished all the education that the village and the vicar combined can give him, insists on following his growing love of Elizabethan poetry to the Reading Room of the British Museum. His stepfather reluctantly permits this for one year, but refuses to finance the venture any longer."

"I really do not think that Mr. Moseley could afford to do so," I interjected.

"I agree with you. If you remember, I told you that the London address which Mr. Moseley gave me was merely an accommodation one. I have been able to discover his reason for this: he was staying in a lodging-house on Tooley Street."

"Impossible, Holmes!" The very thought of a gentleman staying in that area, no matter how briefly, was distressing to me.

"I admit that I was surprised myself. To return to Mr. Raleigh, he refuses to accept the life of a village lawyer that his stepfather urges upon him and instead works in that lawyer's office for a year and then takes a similar post in London."

"Aleck also met and married Winnie," I interposed.

"He did indeed, a young lady who is herself a direct descendant of Sir Walter Raleigh, a fact which she most strangely keeps secret, and who arrives in England with sufficient knowledge of the legacy letter to go at once to the lawyers' office and inquire about it: according to the note made at the time by the clerk and by the records of the steamship company, Miss Hepworth was not in London more than four-and-twenty hours before she called. Though soon employed, she also spends much of her free time reading Elizabethan history at the B.M. and, when her employer is going to the Lake District, prefers to journey to the desolate regions of Nightsead. She is a tall young lady with a contralto voice, capable of acting a man's part in a village pageant."

"She was *not* the red-headed man at the Reading Room," I here interrupted. "That was Dan Thatcher."

"You are positive, Watson?"

I hesitated. "I am positive that it was not Winnie. And nearly positive that it was young Thatcher. Size, hair colour—"

"There are such things as wigs and padding, doctor."

"And his walk? He walked like Dan Thatcher."

"That is far stronger evidence," Holmes agreed, "although not conclusive."

"We know that Dan Thatcher was in London at the time," I reminded Holmes, "he is apparently better educated than one would expect, and his morals are far from the highest—remember his disgusting alliance with Janet."

"I am remembering it. I am also remembering that Mrs. Raleigh most vigorously supported his quest for a London position, even to indicating that she and her husband would divide their own very limited finances with young Thatcher. 'We haven't much, but whatever we have we'll share with Dan.' I believe those were Mrs. Raleigh's words?"

"They were. And very generous," I insisted stoutly, "the expression of a woman of true compassion."

"In fact, of a woman of incalculable worth," Holmes amended with a slight smile. "Quite so, although I cannot help wondering why Mrs. Raleigh feels so committed to assisting young Thatcher. And we must also remember that, though he did not go to the hospital, he was at the restaurant with Mrs. Raleigh and Mr. Moseley when Mr. Raleigh became so ill."

"Have you reached any conclusions as to the cause of Aleck's illness, Holmes?"

"I have, yes. You remember that a Gypsy violinist came over to the table and played?"

"Some American songs for Winnie," I nodded.

"I have questioned him, and he says that Mr. Raleigh drank most of his half glass of wine at a gulp and that there was a white powdery substance floating in it."

"Holmes!"

"I believe the young Gypsy to be telling the truth, Watson. The wineglass was of course smashed in the ensuing commotion when Mr. Raleigh became ill."

"Did the Gypsy not see how the powder came into Aleck's glass?"

"He says that he did not."

"But . . . Winnie did *not* do it, Holmes."

"She has the best motive, Watson."

"But . . . the legacy is only an historic trinket," I offered, lamely enough, "worthless."

"If we all truly believed that, it is strange that we are spending so much time on it, is it not?"

"Yet . . ." I lapsed into a long moment of hard thought. I ended by admitting, "I cannot see what Mr. Moseley would gain from Aleck's death."

"Nor can I."

"As for Dan Thatcher," I went on reluctantly, "he could only lose by it, lose the little help which Winnie and Aleck have promised."

"It was *Mrs.* Raleigh who told you so emphatically that she and her husband would give that help, Watson. Who is to say what the situation would have been had Mr. Raleigh not survived the swallowing of that white powder?"

I stared at Holmes in momentary bewilderment. Then, "*No,*" I objected, loudly. "No, Holmes, it is not so. Winnie is deeply in love with Aleck. The very thought that she would injure him, especially for another man, is utterly repugnant."

"Repugnant ideas are yet sometimes true, doctor, and there has recently been added to the mystery the attack on Mrs. Raleigh herself . . . Let us go on to other facts, merely pausing to note how white and thin Mr. Moseley appeared at the hospital the day of Mr. Raleigh's sudden illness. The occasion of the little luncheon party had been Mr. Raleigh's recent discovery that the name of the firm of lawyers who have perpetual keeping of the legacy letter is that of Sir Walter's mother. Since that time Mr. Raleigh has also found that his ancestor did indeed once have access to booty from a captured Portuguese ship, and he has shown us a true copy of the Raleigh letter."

Here Holmes paused for so long that I finally asked, "Can you still make nothing of that infuriating letter, Holmes?"

"Infuriating is the right word," he replied with a long sigh, "for not only can I *not* make anything of it, I am steadily tormented with the thought that I *should* be able to do so, that I already know the vital clue ... Somehow, Watson, it concerns Nightsead and that confounded little carved frog. No, I do not know how—that is, I am not consciously aware of how—but it does. And that is why I am going to Devonshire. Raleigh was from Devon, you know, as was Lady Raleigh, and ... At any rate, I am going. Would you care to accompany me?"

"No," I returned with considerable honesty, "but I certainly do not intend being left behind."

We spent a week idling about Devon in weather that had suddenly turned chill. East Budleigh, Hayes Barton, over to Compton (the castle most picturesque), off to Plymouth, across to Exeter (the cathedral precinct dwellings very graceful). Small inns, roaring fires, cold coaches, long and colder walks, and the shire's justly famous cream. That to me made up our week, and, until near the end of it, I think that it made up that of Holmes as well.

He had popped in and out of shops, making small purchases which, as often as not, were so completely unwanted that he left them behind at whatever lodging we were inhabiting. He had spent hours in courteous conversation with a large number of people wherever we happened to be, steadily asking casual questions about Sir Walter Raleigh, one of Devon's most famous sons.

He was answered by a large number of stories which, though interesting enough, did nothing to advance the case. We heard again and again of Sir Walter's having first gained the attention of Queen Elizabeth by throwing down his red velvet cloak so she could cross a mud puddle without staining her satin slippers, and we heard the opposing story that he first piqued the queen's interest by taking a ring from his finger and, with the diamond it held, scratching on a window-pane. Curious, the queen approached. Sir Walter had written, "Fain would I climb, yet I fear to fall." The queen, ever quick witted, took the ring from him and completed the couplet with her own challenge: "If thy heart fail thee, climb not at all."

As I say, interesting enough as evidence of the vivid personalities involved—tempestuous queen and ambitious courtier—yet, as far as I could see, helping to solve the legacy mystery not a whit. My thoughts kept straying to my unhappy friends in London, and I think even Holmes' spirits were beginning to flag when we had our first stroke of luck.

We were walking the cold and windy streets of a little town in north Devon when across the way Holmes spotted a stonemason's shop. Like a shot he was off and through the door, and, by the time I had caught up with him, he was already deep in conversation with the lad of the shop, who was displaying a shelf of rock samples.

" 'Tis ca-alled Devo-on ma-arble in the tra-ade, sur," the boy was explaining, "but 'tis no-thing but sa-andsto-one when a-all's sa-aid and do-one."

"When all's said and done," Holmes murmured to me significantly, and even I could see that the block of stone resting in the middle of the shelf was of the same kind as that on which the little frog had been carved and set above the hearth of Nightsead.

"But Holmes," I protested as we made our way back to our inn, "I cannot see that this helps at all."

"The stone is from Devon—is, as I have just been told, one of the most famous exports of the shire—and Sir Walter was from Devon. That is important, Watson, precisely because it is the first bit of solid evidence to connect Sir Walter with Nightsead at all."

"It is not much," I protested.

"It is not," Holmes agreed. "I quite agree with all the criticism in your expression, my dear fellow: I am chasing the wildest of geese. And yet . . ." A long pause while we crossed the square and turned into our inn. "And yet I am more and more tormented by the feeling that I already know the one vital piece of evidence connecting all, and that it is—"

Holmes broke off abruptly, and stood as one transfixed; in fact, I inadvertently bumped into him, so suddenly had he stopped just inside the inn door. To our immediate left was the public room, doing a brisk early evening trade, and immediately adjacent to where we stood a group of husky countrymen were discussing their crops, their families, their animals, their lives with that strangely warm and yet flat accent of Devon.

"Ded you fenesh u-up tha-at fi-eeld, Ra-alph?"

A disgusted and negative growl. "Wo-on't be froo with hit 'tel Forsda-ay or la-ater by the lo-oks of hit. Ter'ble roggy tha-at la-and be."

There was another growl, this time of confirmation, from his mates, and then the voice of the innkeeper, raised in friendly query from behind his bar. "Ded you wa-ant a gla-ass of so-omething, sur?"

Holmes seemed to rouse as from a trance. "Thank you, no. I have already all I need."

Without a word more he bolted up the stairs and, in our joint room, began throwing his few possessions into his bag. "We've just time to catch the evening train, Watson, if we hurry."

"To London?" I hastily opened my own case.

"Of course: there is nothing more for us here. Ring the bell, would you?" He was scribbling on a pad as he spoke. "I want this telegram to go at once."

It was addressed to the British Museum with a prepaid answer to be handed to us at Broxley: "When did wife of Sir Walter Raleigh die?"

"What does it matter when Lady Raleigh died?" I demanded, but not another word would Holmes say until we were safely on the train. Then I repeated my question, and Holmes replied, "Because, if you remember from your own recent reading in Raleigh biographical material, before her marriage Lady Raleigh was a Throckmorton."

"That is important?"

"It is vital. More, remember that puzzling reference in the legacy letter to the writer kissing the lips of the 'mort' lord."

"I cannot see that the precise manner of the caress matters," I objected impatiently.

"If I am right, it matters a great deal. In fact, it explains the 'grate Treshur' of the letter. Have you ever visited Canterbury, Watson?"

"Yes," I retorted, "during my student days. And I have no desire to turn pilgrim again."

"Nor I, for I too once followed the road of Chaucer. Do you remember when Sir Walter was executed, doctor?"

I shook my head.

"In 1618."

"But didn't Queen Elizabeth's reign end about the turn of the century?" I objected.

"In 1603, yes."

"Then Raleigh was not executed during Elizabeth's time!" I exclaimed.

"Certainly not: he had done much to anger the queen, though nothing which would have forced her to send a man she favoured to his death. His trial, his long imprisonment, his temporary release and his execution were all under the suspicious, avaricious, unstable James. Do you remember who ruled after James, Watson?"

"I am hardly that well read in English history, Holmes."

"Yet this is a name that you know well, as does every schoolboy. Who was the only king ever executed in this land?"

"Charles the First!" I exclaimed.

"James' son. Quite right. And do you remember how he was executed?"

"Beheaded, of course," I replied impatiently. "How else would a nobleman of that time be put to death?"

"As you say, how else? Ah, we have stopped at Broxley, and here comes the porter, no doubt with the answer to my telegram."

The answer was duly handed to Holmes, but it received scant attention from either of us, for there was a second telegram, which had been following us from place to place in Devon for the past five days. It was from Aleck and said only, "Janet found murdered in the Nightsead field."

Without a word, Holmes reached up to the rack and grabbed his bag.

"You are going to Nightsead?" My shocked mind was just able to form this assumption.

"I am." Holmes had his cloak over his arm. "Though I am no doubt far too late." He paused with his hand on the carriage door as I too began hastily collecting my few possessions. "Are you sure that you do not prefer to go on to London, Watson? For I warn you, the journey which I shall take to Nightsead will be a difficult one."

"I have never known one to that forsaken spot that was not," I replied and followed Holmes out onto the platform.

Indeed, he had not exaggerated the difficulties ahead of us: five trains were necessary before, as the first of the dawn lit the sky, we climbed stiffly out at Wrinehill, on the far side of Nightsead, where we had weeks earlier been met by a hired horse and gig. Now not even the station-house was open, and we had to leave our bags to the mercy of early rising passers-by.

"It is a goodly climb across the hills," Holmes said quietly, "and yet I dare neither delay longer nor use a more conventional means of approach."

"Then let us start," I replied, "and at least warm our blood by exercise."

"I hardly feel that mine needs warming," Holmes returned, and there was something in his voice which served to make me step out quickly without another word.

In about two hours, with the sky now well light above us, we were working our way around that last rise before the Nightsead field. Once we had reached the top, Holmes paused and, glass to his eye, surveyed the scene. Almost at once we were off again, and certainly the spot we sought was sadly easy to find.

The path from Nightsead reached the crest of the sloping field and there branched into two, one leading across to the Thatchers' farmhouse, the other down over the hills to the village. At the intersection was a little hollow, and there a heavy clump of wild brush grew in straggling profusion. Now these low bushes carried signs of considerable disturbance.

There had earlier been a hard frost, and the dead grasses and light brush had been broken off, squashed, trampled, and generally tossed hither and yon. Over all could be seen the imprints of many boots, some hobnailed, and this sight brought forth a deep sigh of exasperation from my companion.

For some moments he stood surveying that patch of frozen vegetation. "It is clear enough where the body lay," he then observed, pointing with his stick, "for the impression in the grass is still quite clear—I think the night of the murder must have been that of the first frost in the area." Straightening, he surveyed the near and looming coldness of Nightsead: no lights, no sounds, nothing to suggest human habitation, and though this was usual enough with that desolate abode, yet the silent might of the place that morning struck cold to my very soul.

"Mr. Moseley—surely he is not still living there, alone?" I involuntarily asked.

"I should think not," Holmes replied, indifferently, bending to examine the ground more closely. "I expect that the Roundtrees will have asked him to stay with them for a few days . . . There was a struggle. That much is evident—" He broke off abruptly and dropped to his knees.

"Look," he said with quiet exultation, "there, Watson, and there, and there also." He was pointing to something that I could discern only after I too had knelt and lowered my face almost to the frozen ground. A sprinkling of a fine white substance had fallen through the dead brush and lay, much like granular frost, on the dark earth, and with it were a few fragments of what appeared to be clear glass.

"A long shot, doctor, a very long shot." Holmes was using the blade of his pocket-knife to gather the powder and splinters into an envelope. "But what is this?" His probing fingers had parted some further strands of grass and revealed a cork about half an inch in diameter and perhaps two inches long.

"It could have been there for weeks, Holmes."

He shook his head. "Not at all discoloured. In fact, even the end which has been inserted in a container of some kind is nearly as light in shade as the rest of the cork. And," raising it to his nose, "there is no odour of any kind clinging to it—none. Curious. Let us see . . ." He played his lens carefully on the end which, by the marks of pressure, showed that it had indeed filled some receptacle. "A few grains of what appear to be salt."

"Salt?" I ejaculated.

"Table salt, yes." Holmes was gently wrapping the cork in his handkerchief. "We shall certainly keep this most interesting specimen for later examination. Now let us see if there is anything further." A few minutes later Holmes was back on his feet, dusting his hands. "Nothing. If we had been able to have been here earlier . . . Ah well, we must be thankful that we came at all."

By the time we had scrambled back down into Wrine-hill, I was nearly asleep on my feet. Fortunately the station-master's wife took pity on us, letting us into her warm parlour and serving us a most delicious and substantial country breakfast.

Only on the train, now again headed for London, did I finally ask, "Holmes, why was Janet killed?"

"I have far too few facts to be able to answer that yet, doctor."

"Yet you must have some thoughts on the subject?"

"I think that Janet precipitated her own death. She was, apparently, a woman whom it was unsafe to cross too deeply. No, Watson," as I was about to speak again, "we must wait for more facts, facts which I am hoping that Mr. Raleigh will help provide. By the way, here is the answer to that telegram that I sent to the Museum."

It read: "Lady Raleigh died in 1647."

As soon as we arrived in London, Holmes sent a note to Aleck, asking him to call, and this he did early the next day. He looked tired and dispirited, poor fellow, for he had just returned from Janet's funeral.

"How is Winnie?" I asked at once.

"Quite well. That is . . . yes, she's well." He sat down heavily in the visitor's chair, and I knew that the cloud of mutual unease that had fallen on my friends had not yet been dispersed.

"Mr. Raleigh," Holmes leaned forward, "there are details concerning the murder of Janet that I must know." Aleck nodded dumbly. "Who found the body?"

"Dan Thatcher and my stepfather," Aleck replied wearily. "Janet had been visiting the Thatchers, and my stepfather had walked into the village to the Round-trees. He stayed for supper and arrived back at Night-sead around half past ten. He didn't give a thought to Janet—she quite suited herself as to when she came in, you know—and simply went to bed. Then in the morning, when she didn't knock on his door with his tea, he finally got up and went to her cottage. But it was dark and cold, the fire long out, and Janet's bed hadn't been slept in.

"So he did the only thing he could think of and started off towards the Thatchers. He kept on looking ahead for Janet, thinking that she must have stayed overnight for some reason and that she would surely be on her way back to Nightsead by then. But he reached the farm-house with no sign of her, and the Thatchers said that she had left a little after seven the previous evening. Dan started back with my stepfather, looking all the way, and when they came to where the path joins the trail down the Nightsead hill, they . . . they found her."

"How had she been killed?"

"By a blow on the head. In fact, Dr. Leckie said that she must have been dead when she hit the ground. The whole left side of her temple was caved in, and there was a rock near by that . . . that had been the weapon."

"She left the Thatchers a little after seven the previous evening," Holmes repeated, "and it would take her how long to walk to Nightsead?"

"Well under an hour: she was there by eight. You see, Dan Thatcher went with her; he always did if it was dark."

"He escorted her right to her cottage?"

"No, for some reason Janet would never let him do that. But he says that he watched her go in and close the door behind her. Mr. Holmes, the police suspect Dan, and he's innocent. I know it."

Holmes raised his brows. "Dan Thatcher hasn't been arrested, surely?"

Aleck shook his head. "But the police keep questioning him, and it's pretty obvious what they're thinking. Dan's terribly upset, and of course he has contradicted himself in what he's said, anyone might. And . . . all Janet's savings have been stolen. She was like a lot of the country people and wouldn't have anything to do with banks, so she used to keep her bit of money—it was never much, as you can imagine—in a tin hidden underneath a stone of the kitchen hearth. When the police searched the kitchen, they soon found the loose stone and the empty tin, and now they've discovered that Dan is really desperate for money: he wants to start medical studies. Oh, I know it sounds foolish, but it's not. Really it's not, Mr. Holmes: Dan has the brains to do it."

"But of course not the money. How much would Janet have had in the tin?"

Aleck shrugged. "A few pounds, probably. But of course there's no proof of how much there was, and no proof either that Dan didn't think that it was a lot more."

"No woman working at Nightsead could possibly have enough money to be murdered for," I said positively.

Aleck gave a sad little smile. "Unfortunately, there is no reason to believe that the police will think the same. Is there, Mr. Holmes?"

"They can be incredibly foolish," Holmes admitted, "although I should think that even the country police would need better evidence than they seem to have against Dan Thatcher before they would proceed to an arrest."

"If they keep on at Dan," Aleck retorted wearily, "he'll provide the evidence: he's so upset he hardly knows what he is saying. Mr. Holmes, can't *you* do something?"

"What I can do, Mr. Raleigh, be assured that I will," Holmes returned quietly.

There seemed little more to be said. Aleck left shortly thereafter, and Holmes at once went out also. He had not returned at midnight when I retired, but, the next morning as I rang for breakfast, Holmes came out of his room. He looked exhausted, his face white and his eyes dark-ringed, yet there was an air of quiet jubilation about him that was arresting.

"You were out late, Holmes?"

"You might say so, for I have just got in. I went back to Nightsead."

"But why?" I exclaimed. "And at such an hour?"

"The hour was dictated by the fact that I had no excuse to offer to Mr. Moseley should he have found me exploring the cupboards of the Nightsead kitchen."

"You wished to look at Janet's quarters." I felt that I could at least understand this.

But Holmes replied, "Not specifically, no. Not since both the police and Mr. Moseley, and probably Mr. Raleigh and his wife, and perhaps Mrs. Thatcher and even Mrs. Roundtree have all been there. I went to find this." He removed from his pocket a slender hand-kerchief-wrapped package a foot or more long, and produced from it something like a glass bottle, of heavy smoky green glass, made with an unusually long neck and a rounded bottom. It was half full of some white granular substance. "It was already polished clean when I found it," Holmes added, handing the bottle to me, "so we need take no precaution in examining it."

"What on earth is it meant for?" I asked, turning it around in my fingers. "It must fit into a container of some kind, for it most certainly can't be made to stand up on its own, not with that rounded bottom."

"Because it isn't meant to stand," Holmes rejoined. "We poor males are unlikely to be familiar with such an implement, but I'll warrant that Mrs. Hudson" (who was then entering with our breakfast) "will have no trouble in identifying it."

"Why, 'tis a common rolling-pin, sir. For making pastry and such like." She was briskly unloading her tray and had taken no more than a glance at the bottle-like object I held.

"And for rolling out griddle cakes, no doubt?" Holmes murmured with a glance at me.

"Depends on what kind you make, sir. Mine (my

mother's receipt I use) takes a real batter, and you drop 'em right on the griddle from the spoon, but the northern folk, they make 'em stiffer as a rule and roll 'em out. You'll ring when you want your coffee, sir?" And out she went.

"A rolling-pin," I repeated, still looking at the glass container. "That cork you found fitted into the open end?"

"I have yet to try it," Holmes replied, taking his seat at the table, "but I am sure that it will fit very nicely."

"And the white grains on the cork were of course from the substance which is still in the bottle. *Is* it table salt?"

"I have made no tests, but I am informed that salt is the commonly used material. It is simply to allow the cook to adjust the weight of her implement according to her own preference."

"Yet why the long neck?" I asked.

"I really feel that I would like my coffee now," Holmes replied, a small twinkle showing in his tired eyes. "Now, Mrs. Hudson," as she bustled in, "kindly give us a demonstration of how this rolling-pin would be used. I shall just stuff this bit of paper into the open end . . . There you are, Mrs. Hudson."

"Why, there's little enough to the using of it, sir," she said. "You simply take it up, so," grasping the pin by the long neck, which fitted the palm of her hand to a nicety, "and guide it along with your other 'and, so." She made several brisk passes back and forth over our tablecloth, and I could almost see a lump of dough being flattened out by each stroke. " 'Tis a good feeling pin, sir," Mrs. Hudson concluded, putting it carefully back in the middle of the table, "but overlight at the moment for my taste. Perhaps some of the salt was spilled, like, when the cork came out?"

"I think it very probable," Holmes replied gravely. "Thank you, Mrs. Hudson, you have been a great help."

"But, Holmes," I said slowly as the door closed behind our landlady, "surely Janet was killed by a blow from a piece of rock?"

"She was: the police have confirmed that. And in any case one would hardly expect a murderer to extract from the Nightsead kitchen this rolling-pin which, even if filled to the brim with salt, would not weigh more than a couple of pounds, when better weapons would be literally lying all around his feet in the scattered bits of Nightsead rock. I think that, some time after she returned to her kitchen quarters, Janet left again, taking her rolling-pin with her."

"Why ever would she do that?"

"To have an implement with which she was very familiar to use as a weapon."

"Then she *expected* to be attacked?"

"She expected to need just such a weapon as she took. When I found the cork, I of course thought at once of a bottle, but the cork gives no sign of having been in contact with any sort of liquid or vapour. When I found those few grains of salt adhering to the cork, I remembered where I had seen just that kind of cork before: in a rolling-pin."

"Where did you find the pin?"

"Where it belonged, in one of Janet's kitchen cupboards. Next to a flour dredger."

"Then it was returned," I said slowly, "by the murderer."

"I believe so, yes. Certainly it had been wiped until it fairly glistened. Janet's cottage," he added, "as you will remember, has no lock on the door."

"Holmes, is there *nothing* that we can do? For the police are not apt to pay any attention to your discovery of the rolling-pin, are they? And I cannot see that it helps prove Dan Thatcher's innocence, in any case. If indeed he is innocent, and of that I am far from sure."

For a long moment Holmes was silent. "I think," he said at last, "that we had better appeal to Mr. Raleigh to join us in a difficult project in which the final decision should be his."

"And Winnie's," I insisted stoutly, only hoping that I was correct. "Aleck will not leave her out of anything important, I am sure."

"I am afraid that it is I who must insist that Mrs. Raleigh be kept uninformed of our attempt, Watson."

He would say no more.

"Two narrow words: Hic jacet"

Sir Walter Raleigh,
"Apostrophe to Death," *History of the World*

HOLMES, Aleck and I were on our way to Nightsead. In speaking of this journey, Holmes had said little
to my friend, yet Aleck had at once agreed: it was obvious
that he was eager for any errand that would take him,
however briefly, away from London and the unresolved
silence that now lay between him and Winnie. So we were
on our way, not to the village below Nightsead, but to
Wrinehill, on the other side of those steep slopes.

I had questioned the reason for this circumspection.

"It will be better if we attract as little attention as
possible," Holmes had replied.

"Mr. Moseley—" I had begun.

"Is still staying with the Roundtrees. Or so Mr. Raleigh believes."

It had been late afternoon when we had caught the
train, it was now early evening, and for the first time
since we had left London, we had a carriage to ourselves.
Holmes, who had spent the time smoking steadily, at
last put his empty pipe in his pocket, opened the window
wide, and, as the cold air swept cleanly over us, stood
gazing out into the darkness which was rapidly falling

on the world outside. Finally, bringing the window down softly, he returned to his seat and said quietly, "Before we arrive, Mr. Raleigh, we should exchange such information as we have."

"You made some discovery in Devon?" Aleck asked, and his drawn face quickened.

"Rather say that the trip served to jog loose the vital fragment of knowledge that I have possessed all along, Mr. Raleigh. For some time I have amused myself with making a little study of country dialects; I may some day publish a monograph on the subject, for it is certainly a fascinating one."

"Yet what has that to do with the mystery of Nightsead?" I queried.

"Consider the curious spelling of the legacy letter."

"Spelling was not standardized in Elizabethan times, Mr. Holmes," Aleck cautioned.

"Certainly it was not—I believe, of the six unquestioned signatures of Shakespeare, not two are identical—yet I am right, I think, in saying that doubling vowels, as is frequently done in the legacy letter, was not common?"

Aleck paused for thought. "You are right, Mr. Holmes: I can't remember ever seeing that particular oddity so frequently before."

"More, you said that the writing was somewhat sprawling and irregular, in fact not the hand of an educated Elizabethan at all?"

"I did," Aleck agreed, "and I haven't changed my opinion."

"Yet very few of the poorer classes would have been able to write at all, would they, Mr. Raleigh?"

"True. In any case, my legacy letter doesn't *sound* as if it were written by an uneducated person. That last blessing, that almost contemptuous labelling of some royal personage as a fool, that reference to a dear lord with whom an intimate kiss is frequently exchanged, the ownership of the 'Doobel Haart' (whatever that is, it seems of value), and of the 'grate Treshur,' not to mention the clear inference that the writer and recipient of the letter wrote to each other frequently as children: no, the letter is not that of an uneducated person, regardless of the handwriting."

"Then what class of Elizabethan could well have an aristocrat's breeding and spirit without the training that went with it?"

For a moment Aleck stared blankly and then exclaimed, "A woman! An upper class woman! taught to read and write but not much else."

Holmes nodded. "So I believe. More, an upper class woman who came from Devon and who, precisely because she had little formal education, *wrote as she spoke.* 'A laast bless you . . .' " Holmes recited the letter to the end, and, hearing those flat yet rich sounds roll forth, I had to admit that his argument was convincing. "We can go yet further in identifying the lady, for we can presume that she had some intimate connection with your family. The letter, after all, is a Raleigh legacy and is in the keeping of lawyers who bear the name of Sir Walter's mother. Who then wrote the letter?"

"Lady Raleigh," Aleck replied promptly and with conviction.

"So I too believe, not least because she signed her letter *with the childhood device of her family nickname*."

"She was named Elizabeth and called Bess," Aleck began hesitantly and then, his eyes lighting up, exclaimed, "Yes! Why didn't I see it before! Here, Jack," hastily scrawling on an old envelope a copy of the crude drawing from the letter, "that little thing with loops is meant to represent a *bee*, and also naturally the letters *Be*, and those curved lines like parentheses which flank it put together make an *s*. Be-ss—of course!"

"Of course," Holmes agreed. "If the drawing had not been so poor, we would have seen it at once."

"Then to whom was the letter addressed?" I asked eagerly. "To Sir Walter?"

"I believe not," Holmes replied, "for, if I am right, the letter was written late in Lady Raleigh's life, many years after Sir Walter's execution."

"That 'laast bless you' does sound like the final farewell of an elderly person," Aleck agreed, "as does that fond memory of shared childhood days."

"There is also Lady Raleigh's description of her correspondent as one who did ever hold his soul in his own teeth. Is there anyone in Lady Raleigh's family who was particularly independent in religious matters?"

Again Aleck's face lit. "Of course! Her brother Robert. He was in the secret service and, while on a mission in Spain and in spite of the fact that he knew it would end his career, became a Catholic. The queen had to dismiss him from the court, but she may well have secretly admired his courage, for she granted him the deed to Nightsead and its lands—there, Mr. Holmes, that is *my* latest discovery."

Holmes sat back, rubbing his thin hands together in satisfaction. "Capital, Mr. Raleigh, capital! A Catholic owning the ruined monastery of Nightsead, a brother to Lady Raleigh and thus brother-in-law to Sir Walter: that is precisely what completes the picture."

"I cannot see how it completes the picture of that second curious scrawl at the end of the legacy letter," I objected. "How could that rough circle enclosing two smaller circles possibly represent 'Robert' or any nickname for it?"

"His nickname was not from his Christian but from his family name," Holmes replied.

"Was that not Throckmorton?" I asked. "What nickname could possibly come from that?"

"You are forgetting that Lady Raleigh's family came from Devon; you are forgetting that fragment of conversation we overheard in the Devon inn. In her home county, Lady Raleigh's maiden name was pronounced 'Frogmoorton,' and in childhood her brother Robert was undoubtedly called 'Frog' or 'Froggy.' That rough little drawing is meant to represent a frog's big head and bulging eyes."

"Then that little carving above the Nightsead hearth," I began and stopped, for I could go no farther.

"Was done in a block of Devon marble and set above the hearth in the hall of Robert Throckmorton's estate most probably to celebrate the secret marriage of his sister Bess 'Frogmoorton' to her courtier Sir 'Water' Raleigh: a frog in a moor with sea waves underneath."

"The marriage may even have been performed in that hall," Aleck added, "for certainly it was not held at court, and of course the marriage was made many years before Cromwell and the destruction of Nightsead."

"Who was the royal father and son of the legacy letter," I asked, "the father against whom the writer had a heavy charge and the son who, though a fool, had done what he could to help?"

"James the First," Aleck replied promptly, "and Charles the First: if the writer of the letter is Lady Raleigh, that becomes obvious. James not only had Raleigh convicted of treason on trumped up charges, imprisoned for a dozen years and finally executed, he also seized as much of Raleigh's estate as he could and even stripped Nightsead from Lady Raleigh's brother."

"And his son Charles restored them!" I cried.

"Not Raleigh's lands since they had been removed legally as the property of an executed traitor, but Nightsead had been taken on no good grounds, taken to be given as yet another gift to the king's favourite, the Duke of Buckingham. After Buckingham's assassination, Charles, by then on the throne, returned Nightsead to Robert Throckmorton."

"When did this seizure and restoration of Nightsead take place, Mr. Raleigh?" Holmes asked.

"It was conveyed to Buckingham in the early 1620s and was returned to Robert in 1646, during Charles' lengthy struggle with Parliament—during the period, in fact, when he most showed himself to be indeed a 'pooar roial fuule.' "

"So for a period shortly after Raleigh's death to not long before Lady Raleigh's, Nightsead was not in the hands of her family, indeed was in the possession of one who, as a favourite of the king, could be said to be her family's enemy? And by the time Nightsead had been returned to Lady Raleigh's brother, it had been gutted by Cromwell's soldiers? Yes." Holmes nodded, and, leaning back and placing his fingertips together, recited from the legacy letter, " 'Keep the Doobel Haart hoole and whaar hit is I praie you and at the laast let mi grate Treshur bee there also.' "

"Holmes, do you mean," I nearly rose in my sudden excitement, "that you expect to find that 'Doobel Haart' at Nightsead?"

"And Lady Raleigh's 'grate Treshur,' " Holmes replied. "I do indeed. Why else are we making this journey?"

"The treasure—it's behind that little carved frog!" I cried.

Holmes shook his head. "Remember the wording of the letter. After giving her directions to put the 'Doobel Haart' and her 'grate Treshur' together, Lady Raleigh adds, as if in explanation of what she has requested, 'foor you ded ever hold your Sole in your owne Teeth and Hee was ever with God whaatever thei ded sai.' If you have a recently ruined monastery in your family, a monastery owned by a brother who became a Catholic during a belligerently Protestant time, and if your executed husband had been falsely labelled an atheist by his enemies, where would you, a lady whose spirit was equal to that of both brother and husband, choose as a hiding place for something most precious to you?"

"Under the high altar," Aleck replied at once, and, the more I thought, the more I agreed.

"But what hope have we of locating the old altar?" I asked dismally. "It will be buried under the worst of that pile of fallen rock."

"We have some guidance," Holmes returned, "for the Cistercians put their altars on the highest point of the site."

"And we will have some help," Aleck added firmly. "I wired Dan Thatcher to meet us below the Nightsead hill."

There was a moment's silence. Then Holmes, with a soft sigh, murmured, "Perhaps, after all, it is better this way."

Again Holmes had arranged for a horse and gig to be ready for us, this time with equipment from the local smith packed under the seat.

"What possible excuse did you give for wanting all this?" I wondered aloud as we trotted briskly away into the night, lanterns swinging.

"The best excuse of all," Holmes replied drily. "A five-pound note."

We once more made the journey to the bottom of the rise before Nightsead, and there left the horse. As we rounded the edge of the field, there was a slight movement in the bushes ahead, and Dan Thatcher stepped out. He touched Aleck gently on the shoulder and silently fell into step with us. His very presence made me uneasy, for I was still certain that he was the man I had seen in the Reading Room and thus was probably also the fellow who had tried to impersonate Aleck on the morning of his twenty-first birthday. Yet, eyeing his strong frame, I knew that we would be glad of his hard muscle in the task that lay ahead of us.

There was a waning moon that night, and we had brought the lanterns with us. With these we surveyed our task: a hopeless one it seemed to me, for that pile of fallen rock stretched out before us in all directions, and at its thickest was well above a man's height. Holmes, however, produced a metal tape, and with that we fairly quickly ascertained the approximate centre point of the intersection of nave and transepts: here where the side arms had crossed the body of the church was the most likely place for the old high altar.

We were fortunate in that, whatever the method of destruction used by Cromwell's misguided men, at this point the force seemed to have caused the rock to fall outward so that few of the larger blocks were heaped here. Yet even so the labour was daunting, and without Holmes' uncanny knowledge of how the rocks could best be shifted, we would have been quickly doomed.

As it was, Aleck worked like a demon, Dan Thatcher seemed tireless, and Holmes displayed a strength which was a revelation to me. I, though I insisted on doing my share of the brute work, had to admit that I was not up to the sustained labour of my fellows, and was more often given the task of wedging and balancing with the crowbar while the others manoeuvred yet another huge fragment of stone aside.

Perhaps because I was less involved in the physical labour, I was increasingly conscious of those huge standing structures of Nightsead looming still and near, menacingly so as it seemed to my heated mind. After my carefree times with Aleck among these stones of his strange old home, I had unconsciously come to accept the desolate grandeur as something as natural as the barren hills which surrounded us. Now as never before I felt a watching hostility beating like a live thing from within those massive walls, and the more I tried to ignore the sensation, the more it grew until I alternately sweated and shivered with ignoble fear at our secret trespass.

Finally, when I, at least, felt that I could go on no longer, we came to it, a slab unearthly white in the midst of those shadowed rocks: marble. Chipped, dirty, cracked and fallen, but yet undeniably the high altar-stone of the ruined church.

For several moments we stood, filthy, exhausted, and simply gazed. Through my excited mind flitted a vision of those who had once chosen to live here, plainly robed figures who had, however mistakenly, believed, as they saw the simple wine and bread elevated, that they were beholding the perpetual miracle of Christ's redemptive suffering.

It was Holmes who broke the spell, and he spoke urgently. "We must hurry, Mr. Raleigh, for who knows how much time we have, or indeed how much work is yet before us?"

Without a further word we began again. Aleck and Dan Thatcher seized the crowbars, Holmes used all his might to steady the stone, and I kept throwing wedges underneath. So we moved the slab off its broken foundation and slid it into rest against the nearby pile of rock. Below gaped a dark space.

"Well?" Aleck had dropped to his knees and, trembling, seemed unable to do more. It was Holmes who, stretching full length, reached down into the blackness.

Dirt and debris flew away from his fingers, and he murmured, "There is something . . ." Then he lifted, both arms extended into the shadows, and in his hands a cracked and blackened box, the size of a small cradle, was lifted. As he turned to place the casket in Aleck's arms, for a moment rich carvings and embossed metal gleamed through the clinging curtain of earth.

"Come, Mr. Raleigh." Holmes was on his feet. "Whatever the contents, this is your legacy. Take it, and let us go."

"No." Aleck had remained on his knees and was sliding quick fingers over the casket. "It has been here all these years, it will be opened here." Even as he spoke, the top of the box fell away; inside was another box, of some heavy-looking metal. I was reaching for a pick, but Aleck shook his head. "The lock's broken," he explained softly, and flung open the lid. With gentle hands he lifted a blackened and shapeless object, something wrapped in layers of cloth.

"Is that all, Mr. Raleigh?" Holmes asked.

"That is all. The box is empty now."

"Then bring what you have in your hands, and *let us go*. Quickly."

But Aleck, still crouching among the Nightsead rock, was already unwrapping yards of material from the rough ball that he held. At first it seemed as if the material was burlap or canvas; only as the long strip fell away did I gradually realize that the dirt and decay of the centuries had had their way, and that the wrapping was fine white wool, lined with ivory silk. Still layer upon layer Aleck unwound, and smaller and smaller the object in his hands grew. Now it was no larger than a man's two fists . . .

Aleck suddenly looked up at Holmes, and his hazel eyes were wide and dark. "Did you know that the earliest reference I have been able to find of this property's being called Nightsead was in 1623? Five years after Raleigh's execution?"

"I am not surprised," Holmes replied. "Country people usually have some basis for a belief firmly held, and those of this area have long insisted that Nightsead was associated, not with Lady Raleigh's brother, but with Sir Walter himself."

Aleck unwrapped the last strands of cloth. As he did

so, something small and heavy fell to the ground, fell nearly unnoticed, for in his suddenly still hands Aleck held the skull of Sir Walter Raleigh.

Skull? No, the noble head which the miraculous kindness of Nature had mummified so that the brown skin yet held whole and smooth to the bone, the eyes in the soft light of the lantern appeared but recently closed, the greying hair swept back from the high brow, and under the straight nose the curve of the lips was yet firm and proud—lips which, years after the death of her "dere mort Loord," Lady Raleigh had continued in her deep love and mad loneliness to kiss.

"Nightsead, you see," Holmes murmured quietly. "*Knight's head.* What fell to the ground, Mr. Raleigh?"

"What? Oh." Aleck spoke as one awakening from deep sleep. "There *was* something . . ." He fumbled at his feet and then moved his hand out into the light of the lantern.

We could only stare, stunned.

Two huge rubies, each the length of a man's finger, each forming in its uncut state half of a single heart made from an intricate filigree of blackened gold: the "Doobel Haart" of Lady Raleigh's letter, kept "hoole" as she had instructed.

"It *is* a treasure of incalculable worth," I had started to exclaim, but my words were cut off.

"It is indeed, Dr. Watson. And *mine.*"

We had all frozen, caught in the circle of light from the lantern. Ivor Moseley stood among the rocks a few feet from us, his hands holding that gun from his wardrobe and pointing it right at Aleck.

"You have no hope of getting away with this, Mr. Moseley." It was Holmes who spoke, dispassionately.

"I think that I have, Mr. Holmes," he replied, and I shrank from the sound of rigid control in Moseley's voice. "You see, Aleck is going to be gagged and to have his hands tied behind him by our good doctor—I don't know what your medical skill is, Dr. Watson, but I am sure it is up to that—and then Aleck and the treasure are going with me in that gig that you have left so conveniently below the hill. You will of course do nothing to pursue me, for at the first sign that I am being followed, Aleck will die—I will have no choice. Should you take the sensible course of letting me go my way, Aleck will be deposited by some suitably lonely road; by the time he has made his presence known, I will be gone beyond your reach. Understand that I have planned such an escape, in infinite variations, for a long time: I see no reason now to doubt my success."

"Why did you not move before?" Holmes' voice was calmly conversational, though I could catch a glimpse of his eyes, glinting like steel in the fragmented light of the lanterns.

"You know why very well, Mr. Holmes. Over twenty years ago I came to Nightsead with a certain knowledge gained from the scatter-brained memories of my wife; one more vital piece of the mystery the very appearance of Nightsead gave me; other information I have been able to gather through the years—those long years of unutterable boredom! The hours I spent in that miserable Reading Room, the even longer hours I spent poring over those old texts: all to try to master every detail of that most tiresome of periods. For how could I tell what fragment of history might prove the vital clue to the Raleigh legacy? What else could I do, I who did not have access to the legacy letter?

"The rest of my knowledge I have garnered only by following my dear stepson's footsteps; it has necessitated my keeping on sickeningly warm terms with him and that sharp jade of a wife of his, but I have endured that as I have all else. And, I admit, this last stroke—which, I think, is at least partly yours, Mr. Holmes—I had not anticipated, or you would have found nothing for your labours. I have merely been on the watch for you to make some move, and soon: once Janet was dead, I knew that my time was short. For you are beginning to acquire a reputation in some quarters, Mr. Holmes, and I admit that I was afraid of Aleck's association with you."

"Did you attack Mrs. Raleigh because you feared her?" Holmes asked calmly.

Aleck cried out, but Moseley's cold voice showed no tremor. "How else could I stop her and Aleck? Two of them, both residing in London, the girl free to spend as much time as she wished delving into old documents and histories—how could I hope to follow as quickly? I planned to put a crimp in their work on the Raleigh biography, and if I had killed the girl . . ." He shrugged.

"Janet. You killed Janet." Dan Thatcher's voice rang out harshly, and his convulsive move towards Moseley was terrifying in its silent cry of deep and bitter rage.

"Steady, Dan." Aleck had grasped him with his free hand. "That's not the way."

"No," Moseley calmly agreed, "it is not. For if I have to shoot at all, I will have to shoot several times, will I not? And then to take my chances on making an escape. Quite good chances, really, considering how long it would take the country people to understand what had happened, or the country police to organize an attempt to stop me. As for Janet, certainly I removed her out of my path: she gave me no choice, the blackmailing old bitch. But I repeat that I wish no harm to anyone; I merely wish to claim what is mine."

"Yours?" Aleck exclaimed, his fingers instinctively tightening on the gold-encased rubies.

Moseley laughed, shortly and contemptuously. "I am certainly not referring to that hideous leftover from your revered ancestor, Aleck. Leave that here by all means; I have no doubt that Mr. Holmes will take care of it for you—he seems to have a penchant for oddities. It is the double heart of rubies which is mine, and, yes, *mine by right*. Why else did I marry your hag of a mother but for a chance of discovering the Raleigh legacy? Why else have I borne the wasting of the years of my own youth, waiting and striving to pick up some crumbs of knowledge from you about that letter? You who were able to see the letter whenever you wished— you do not know what it was like to be tormented by un-

availing ignorance, to have to fumble on in the dark."
Moseley's voice had risen, and he abruptly broke off,
clamping his lips shut as if aware that he was in danger
of losing the control that was vital to him.

"You also killed Mr. Raleigh's mother." Holmes' indifferent tone made this a mere statement of fact.

"I do not know how you deduced that, Mr. Holmes,"
Moseley's voice was again calm and cold, "but, yes, certainly I did. Once she had given me access to her miserably small estate and my chance at discovery of the
Raleigh legacy, what use was she to me? Pregnant too:
I could not endure *that*. And yet her condition served a
purpose, for it blinded all to what I had to do."

To me, this was the most frightening moment of all:
the final revelation of the mind of a madman, coolly de-
fending acts impossible to justify, to speak of without
a shudder.

"But enough of this. Put that jewel on this rock,
Aleck." The old altar-stone, pushed aside from its foundation, lay between Moseley and his stepson, and as he
spoke he tapped it imperiously with one foot.

Aleck flung back his head. "You want these rubies?
They *are* pretty, aren't they?" Slowly he raised his hand,
and the glow as his fingers moved through the lantern's
light was hypnotizing. "You want them, stepfather,
woman attacker, murderer? Then ... *come and get
them*." And he remained statue still, the rubies a ball of
fire in his outstretched hand.

For a long, breathless moment there was silence. Then
Moseley laughed, short, hard, contemptuous. "You

early learned not to cross me, Aleck; don't forget that lesson now. Do—"

With a vicious snap of his wrist Aleck sent the heavy jewel flying right into Moseley's face, a blazing prism that smashed against his eyes. The man jerked back, his gun discharged with a horrible roar, and I felt the wind of the shot brush my face. But even as Holmes sprang up, Dan Thatcher threw himself at Moseley.

There was a confused wrestling in the dark, with Holmes shouting to me to direct the light of the lantern, Aleck frantically stumbling up over the rocks, and then, again, came the roar of the gun.

Moseley stumbled, staggered, and fell, the gun crashing from his hands, and young Thatcher remained, his breath coming in long gasps, standing above him.

How long we remained so I do not know, or how long we would have, except for Holmes.

"It's over," he said quietly and decisively. "It's all over. Isn't it, Mrs. Raleigh?" He spoke into the dark beyond our small circle of light.

"Yes, Mr. Holmes, it is." To my utter astonishment, Winnie stepped forward, her skirts looped to her boot-tops, a pocket lantern in her hand. She went at once to Aleck and put her arms around him, and, stretching out her hand, pulled Dan to their side.

"When you asked me if I had ever been to Canterbury, Holmes, you were thinking of the naturally mummified head of Thomas à Becket on display there."

"I was, yes. If such a relic of Sir Walter were buried at

Nightsead, it would make sense not only of the name of the ruin, but of the real puzzle of Lady Raleigh's letter: how she was able to kiss the lips of her poor 'mort' lord nearly thirty years after his execution."

We were back in our Baker Street sitting-room; it was a fortnight since the events I have last recorded. The first moments I only dimly remember: Holmes holding the lantern for me as I quickly ascertained that the second shot from Moseley's gun had indeed killed him; Dan Thatcher, still silent and rigid, with Aleck's arm across his shoulders and Winnie clasping his hand and speaking softly and steadily to him. Then our hasty filling in of the gaping hole with whatever rubble came to hand, the replacement of the stone, and our silent departure.

We stopped at the Nightsead stream and helped Dan Thatcher, now shaking uncontrollably, to cleanse himself of Ivor Moseley's blood. Fortunately while labouring over that pile of rock, he had thrown aside his coat, and we soon had him presentable enough for him to make his way home. This Holmes insisted on, and, after a few moments in which Aleck strenuously objected, insisting that he wasn't going to leave Dan, we all agreed, and we saw him slip into the dark farmhouse unnoticed.

As it happened, it was Mr. Thatcher who, later that morning, found the body: uneasy over the two shots he had dimly heard during the night, he had risen at dawn to make a search of the area. The police rapidly came to the conclusion that Holmes had anticipated: that

Moseley had heard some tipsy farm fellows playing the fool among the Nightsead rocks (Aleck confirmed that this did occasionally happen) and that he had taken his gun out in an attempt to scare them away. Having loosed one shot which effectively scattered the intruders, he was then believed to have stumbled and discharged the gun against his own body, and the police accordingly had no lasting interest in the event.

I, however, still felt surrounded by fragments that I was unable to fit into a whole. "When did you first suspect Moseley, Holmes?"

" 'Suspect' is too strong a word for my first feelings about Ivor Moseley, Watson. Rather, I was curious and became more so, especially when during our first interview he suddenly fell silent and I looked up to find him sitting bolt upright while his eyes travelled between your ulster on the coat-rack, your pipe on the mantelpiece, and your gold-headed cane in the corner."

For a moment I surveyed these homely possessions. "I suppose," I said slowly, "that they are all rather distinctive in one way or another."

"They are, yes. Anywhere in the world they would proclaim to me, 'Watson!' "

"And they are all possessions that I have had for some time, in fact since my student days. So Moseley would be familiar with them."

"Which made it all the stranger that when he saw them he did not exclaim, 'Why, do you know my old acquaintance, Jack Watson?' The fact that he did not and indeed almost immediately ended our interview puzzled me, for I could see no innocent explanation for such behaviour."

"Why did you not tell me of this, Holmes?"

"Precisely, my dear fellow, because I felt that there was indeed a mystery surrounding Ivor Moseley and that you could well be one of my chief means of solving it—provided that you remained unprejudiced. Take your pipe from the mantelpiece, Watson, for I have a lengthy tale to reveal.

"You remember that little sketch of a corner of a roof and a window that Moseley made while he was talking to me? (Evidence of a nervous mind, by the way, doctor, and thus in itself interesting.) We agreed that the drawing showed a skill that neither you nor I possessed, and yet, the more I considered it, the less was I satisfied that it had been done by an artist. It lacked what I might call pictorial quality, that mute distortion of reality which a creative mind imposes upon a subject, the result of a particular and private vision: in short, the sketch was that of the artisan, not the artist. And, once I thought of it, that block printing of the copy of the Raleigh letter which Moseley presented to me showed the training of one used to preparing blueprints.

"I accordingly presented my problem to the editor of *The Architect*, and he, possessed of that encyclopaedic memory which seems to be the prime requisite for such people, soon had unearthed sufficient information for me to be able to pursue my inquiries elsewhere.

"Ivor Moseley was not only trained in architecture,

he was virtually born into it. His family had been engaged in that profession for years out of number, but, as is so often the case with old families, was dying out. Ivor was the only child of aged parents, and, inheriting a business in which he had no interest when he was little more than a youth, he proceeded to mortgage away his birthright in order to pursue the pleasures of London. When his money was gone and his credit exhausted, he was forced to retreat to the Continent.

"You may remember that some weeks ago I absented myself for a few days. I went to Baccarat, to find the photographer's shop where the wedding picture of Moseley and Mr. Raleigh's mother was taken, through that shop the area where the newly married couple had briefly resided, and through that a few people who had known them.

"I discovered that Mr. Raleigh's mother seems to have been nearly bereft of that essential commodity called common sense: even as a not particularly young widow, she loved light society, and she chattered endlessly about the fabulous treasure of Sir Walter Raleigh's which her boy would inherit if only someone could decipher the legacy letter.

"Moseley was by then in truly desperate financial straits, and he had a gambler's heart. He pursued and won the feckless woman, and quickly persuaded her to make her small estate, which unfortunately had been left in her own control, over to him. (Nightsead itself was entailed and therefore safe.) What capital Moseley could turn into cash he did, took it to the gambling tables, and lost. Naturally, for he was neither a skilled nor a patient player.

"Left with only a very small income, he was forced to retreat with his wife, by this time pregnant, and her child to Nightsead. But before they left Baccarat he visited the glassworks there and secretly filled a vial with arsenic, much used in that manufacture."

"You do not know that, Holmes," I protested. "You cannot."

"I know that Moseley was at the glass plant, for he signed the visitor's book, a separate signature between that of two groups: no doubt he chose that position so that he would be less easily noticed. And I know that the white powder that fell among the bushes when Janet was killed was arsenic, for I have analysed it. The rest, I think, is justifiable assumption."

"What made you suspect that Moseley had killed Aleck's mother?"

"Any time a pregnant woman, some twenty years older than a husband whom she has recently married, dies in a remote country place, with symptoms which could well be from arsenic, and the husband has earlier had the opportunity to obtain a small quantity of that poisonous metal, I would be suspicious," Holmes replied drily, "and I was in this case. Moseley quickly removed his wife from his path: as he so bluntly said, what further use was she to him?

"Her child, though, was a different proposition. Moseley had already written the lawyers, asking what would happen to the legacy letter should all heirs die, and had been told that the letter would then revert to the Crown: Mr. Raleigh's survival was thus assured, for only through his stepson could Moseley hope to learn the all important wording of the letter. So Moseley was forced to lay a double plan: while he waited those long years for his stepson's majority, he would make himself as expert in the details of Elizabethan history as he could, and he would keep Mr. Raleigh as generally ignorant as possible."

"Yet he paid for Aleck to have private instruction from the vicar," I protested.

"No, Watson, he did not. I have recently paid a short visit to the village and made some discreet inquiries: the kindly vicar, concerned about young Mr. Raleigh's isolation at Nightsead, not only insisted on his attending school, but gave him lessons himself without charge. This Moseley had to accept, for to refuse would have laid him open to serious suspicion and even possible prosecution, but he very carefully kept under lock and key in his room all the books which he had inherited through his wife from Mr. Raleigh's father."

"Aleck's father!" I exclaimed.

"Certainly. He had read Elizabethan history at Oxford, and loved the period so much that he not only kept his old texts, including books of poetry that he had bought purely for enjoyment, but purchased the leading writings in the field as they came out. Moseley thus acquired a good basic library in the field, a library which he safeguarded from his stepson even to the removal of flyleaves from the books, flyleaves which undoubtedly contained the signatures of the previous owner. (Moseley also, by the way, made free with the clothing left by his predecessor, not from choice, but from genuine penury.)

"It was the disruption of his careful scheme that made Moseley react so violently when he caught his young stepson not only in his room but reading one of his books. He at once gave the boy a belting that completed his alienation, an alienation that Moseley quickly realized and feared: at all costs he had to remain good friends with Aleck ever to have a chance of learning more about the legacy letter. So he gave the boy all the books of poetry that he had, no doubt judging them harmless nonsense, and later reluctantly agreed to Mr. Raleigh's spending a year in London to further his poetry studies.

"All this time Moseley had kept on relentlessly following his plan. He not only pored over those old Elizabethan histories until he must have virtually memorized them, he made periodic trips of his own into London in order to spend hours in the Reading Room himself, striving to keep up with recent developments in Elizabethan research as it was reported in *The Times*."

"So that was why he made those weekly trips to the Roundtrees!" I exclaimed.

"That was why: where else would new discoveries, by

the amateur or the professional scholar, be faithfully reported? Once Mr. Raleigh moved to London, however, Moseley was forced whenever he went himself to the B.M. to don the disguise that he had originally assembled when, pretending to be his stepson, he had called on the lawyers who kept the legacy letter: though the lawyers did not know Mr. Moseley by sight, there was no possibility that in his own person they would take him for a young man just turned one-and-twenty. Though they did not guess that their caller was in disguise, they were uneasy about the poor means of identification that he offered, a few commonplace items that he had stolen from his stepson, and fortunately refused to allow him to see the legacy letter. I was suspicious as soon as I heard the description of the caller, for full cheeks, a beard and moustache, and a florid complexion are all most easy to assume, and he kept his gloves on, even though he had to handle some small pieces of paper: again, his hands were not those of a youth just reaching his majority."

"Moseley succeeded in forcing Aleck back to Nightsead," I recalled, "only to have him meet Miss Hepworth, and that was to prove disastrous for Moseley."

"Quite so, although at the time he was highly relieved to see his stepson's interest in the young lady, for he expected that marriage to the penniless girl would at last force Mr. Raleigh into the Roundtree office. Instead, Miss Hepworth briskly rearranged Mr. Raleigh's life so that they both moved to London, and with his

[173]

wife to assist his labours, Mr. Raleigh not only pressed on with his private research but, again through his wife's intermediacy, was invited to write a new biographical sketch of Sir Walter Raleigh, thus concentrating his interest on that figure and raising the legacy letter, which he had come to think of as a mere family oddity, to new importance.

"Moseley began to panic. He had begun well in the lead: not only well read in the basic texts of Elizabethan history, but from his architectural training he had at once guessed Nightsead's monastic origin; the records that I eventually found, he had traced years ago. Yet he had not the mind of the scholar and, in spite of all the studies that he forced himself to undergo, he made no new discoveries.

"Secure in the happiness of his own marriage, Mr. Raleigh was now casually courteous to his stepfather, and, encountering him just after he had himself discovered that the maiden name of Raleigh's mother was the same as that of the firm which was in perpetual charge of the legacy letter, promptly told him. Frantic to slow his stepson's seemingly inexorable advance, Moseley quickly decided on a dangerous venture. He invited Mr. Raleigh and his wife to luncheon."

"Why include Winnie?"

"She was vital to his plan. That Dan Thatcher was with her and thus had to be included in the invitation was awkward, but could not be avoided. Moseley led the way to a restaurant where he knew there was a Gypsy

musician; by inviting him to play for Mrs. Raleigh—
a strange act for a man as near penniless as Moseley,
for he would of course be obliged to tip the fellow—he
distracted attention long enough for him to slip a little
of that vial of arsenic that never left his possession into
Mr. Raleigh's glass."

"Surely this is mere speculation, Holmes?"

"Far from it. I have made a little investigation into
the background of the young Gypsy; he has good reason
to wish to avoid the close attention of the police, and
because of that had been badly upset by Mr. Raleigh's
sudden illness. When I assured him that I was his best
protection against the men in blue (adding a large tip
to my words) and also threatened to call the nearest
constable if he remained obdurate, he quickly revealed
all. Including the fact that it was Moseley himself who
insisted upon taking the wine away with him; he of
course knew that it would be questioned as a possible
cause of Mr. Raleigh's illness, and hoped, by producing
a perfectly normal bottle, to quieten the topic."

"Yet at the hospital Moseley seemed truly concerned
about Aleck," I questioned.

"Indeed he was, for he feared that, instead of making
Mr. Raleigh merely ill, he might have killed him, and
that would end for all time any hope Moseley had of
obtaining a true copy of the legacy letter. All he had
yet were the fragments which his wife had told him of
what she remembered from what her first husband had
told her and a quickly scribbled version that he secretly

took down one day at Nightsead when Mr. Raleigh, unaware of his stepfather's near presence, paraphrased the legacy letter to Miss Hepworth."

"That was how Moseley obtained that copy he brought to you!" I exclaimed.

"That was how, and it marked how frantic Moseley was becoming that he would approach a private investigator. He withdrew the copy as soon as he could once he realized that you and I shared quarters, for he intended controlling the amount of information that I had: he did not wish to reveal, for instance, that the legacy was not in his family at all but in that of his stepson."

"Did you ever really suspect Dan Thatcher, Holmes?"

"He had to be considered. He was present at the luncheon party when Mr. Raleigh was poisoned, and certainly he could have been the man who attempted to impersonate Mr. Raleigh on the morning of his birthday: he is naturally red-headed and of a florid complexion, could easily have added a beard and moustache, and is a big fellow, one who could readily be taken for a few years older than he is. As for the legacy, he could have learned of that from Janet, indeed could have been working with her on some secret scheme of their own to try for the Raleigh treasure. For there was serious need for money there, and Dan Thatcher has known for years who were his real parents: Janet and Moseley—you yourself noted the likeness in the walk of father and son."

I could only stare, speechless.

"On my recent brief visit to the village," Holmes continued, "I had a few quiet words with Dan Thatcher. He informed me that no one had ever told him of his parentage, but that, since he was born there, the whole area naturally suspected the truth, and it was impossible for him not to have grown up with rumours in his ears, rumours which the Nightsead isolation kept from reaching Mr. Raleigh during the same years. These, however, Mrs. Raleigh heard while she was with the Roundtrees; in her brisk honesty she at once told Mr. Raleigh and, asked point blank, Dan Thatcher told the whole story to them."

"That was why they wished to help him?"

"That was why. Knowing that her son had certainly somehow learned the truth, of late when they were alone Janet had openly expressed her affection for him, and he, a most understanding young fellow, accepted it. Dan, of course, had always been the most important person in Janet's life: she gave the kindness that she could not lavish on him to Mr. Raleigh, but her heart remained with her own lad, growing up at the Thatchers. This she indicated by the name she gave him."

"Dan, not Daniel?"

"As recorded in Genesis, Jacob's wife Rachel, distressed that she has no children, gives her husband her maid in order to have children by her; the first is a boy, and Rachel rejoices: 'God hath judged me, and hath given me a son.' That was how Janet felt, the woman

[177]

who, though a respectably brought up Scot, had run away from a brutal husband and ended by having a child by her master.

"Moseley had always refused to acknowledge Dan—he had no affection in his nature and certainly no desire for added responsibility—but in order to keep Janet quiet and in his service (in all senses) at Nightsead, he promised that he would see the boy educated and provided for. He did pay a pittance for Dan to have special lessons with the vicar; no doubt that for some years satisfied Janet, for even Mr. Raleigh had no more.

"Recently, though, Dan had finished all schooling that the village and the vicar together could give him, and Janet began pressing Moseley to live up to his promise to see to the young man's future. Whether or not Moseley had ever intended doing so is, I fear, doubtful; certainly by this time he had been forced to dip into his very scant capital in order to live in London as much as he was, and he avoided giving Janet a definite answer.

"She finally urged Dan to speak to his father himself; this Dan did on the afternoon of Janet's death, making a late afternoon trip to Nightsead to do so. Moseley bluntly refused, pointing out to Dan that he had no proof of his paternity, nor Janet any of Moseley's promise. Janet had already gone to tea at the Thatchers in order to let Dan speak to Moseley unhindered; as he escorted her back to Nightsead, Dan told her of Moseley's total rebuff. Furious, Janet vowed that she would 'make him pay, fair or foul,' but by the time she reached Nightsead Moseley had left for the

Roundtrees. After Dan had returned to his farm home, Janet deliberately took her rolling-pin from the cupboard and went out to lie in wait for her master, hiding in those bushes where the path divides."

"But what could she hope to gain?" I asked. "Not the bit of money in his pockets, surely? That couldn't possibly be enough to help Dan."

"Moseley carried something of much greater value to him than his few shillings: that vial of arsenic that he had obtained at Baccarat—he had murdered once, knew that he would do so again should his scheme ever seem seriously threatened, and so guarded that vial very carefully. That was what I had hoped to find in his room at Nightsead, although I guessed that Moseley would probably keep it on his person at all times."

"And Janet knew of the vial?"

"She certainly would know of it, even if she knew only that it was for some reason precious to Moseley: remember that for some twenty years she had been both general servant of Nightsead and its master's mistress. Undoubtedly she planned to stun Moseley, remove the vial, and retreat to the Thatchers, leaving a note in his pocket saying that he could have the vial back and her silence by providing for Dan.

"But Moseley was too strong for her. In the struggle the vial was dropped and crushed and Janet's fate sealed: she knew too much and she had become too desperate. Moseley snatched up a piece of the Nightsead rock and killed Janet with one blow. He then removed as much of the broken vial and its spilled contents as he could find, and returned to Nightsead to steal her savings, as much to have the money as to cast suspicion on Dan."

"Janet couldn't possibly have had much savings," I protested. "She undoubtedly had paid the Thatchers for their care of Dan all the years."

"If her savings were only shillings, they would yet have been worth the taking to Moseley: he had been financially reduced not only to living in a seamen's lodging-house on Tooley Street whenever he was in London, but to starving himself to near emaciation in a desperate effort to remain in the city as long as he could. But what is this, Watson? Footsteps on our stairs?"

"Winnie!" I exclaimed, jumping to my feet as she entered. "There is nothing wrong, surely?" For her little face was unwontedly serious.

"Not with me at any rate," she responded with a smile, sinking gracefully into the visitor's chair, "but I feel that I owe Mr. Holmes an explanation."

"You do not, Mrs. Raleigh."

"Yet you did at one time suspect me of having poisoned Aleck, did you not?"

"Why do you think that?"

"Because you must have," Winnie replied frankly. "After all, I was there at that restaurant, sitting at a small table right next to Aleck, and I *am*, after all, the next heir to the Raleigh legacy. Which," she added, "I think you already know, Mr. Holmes, for I have learned from friends that there have been some inquiries about my mother's family in America."

"My American correspondent has been clumsy," Holmes remarked, "a problem with amateurs. You are at least right, Mrs. Raleigh, in assuming that you were a puzzle to me. Why did you keep your family background a secret?"

"Well, I grew up on my mother's stories of her historic ancestry, and for years the legacy letter has figured large in my mind. I was determined to find out more some day, and so when I was left alone and had my living to make, I came right over and started my inquiries."

"You already knew about Nightsead?" Holmes asked.

"Oh yes, and knew that in some unknown way it was part of the legacy mystery; that was why I took the first opportunity to see it for myself. But I didn't want people to know what I was up to—if there was anything to find I intended doing that myself—but then I met Aleck and," with a charming blush, "that was that."

"Why didn't you confide the reason for your interest to him?" I asked.

"Oh, Doctor Jack, how could I? He would have felt that I was interested in him only because I was interested in the legacy, that I hoped to move closer to the Raleigh treasure by marrying him. Aleck had had such an awfully lonely childhood, and he trusted me so much, I couldn't let him think that—not for a moment. Have you ever fallen in love, Mr. Holmes?"

"That is one disaster which I have so far been spared," Holmes replied gravely.

"Oh, you can joke about it, but when it happens to you, it's *no* joke, I can assure you. Before I knew it, I was head over heels, and when I found that so was Aleck with me, nothing else mattered: I just pushed all thoughts of my family to the background. And naturally the longer I kept quiet, the more impossible it was to speak. And then when I came to after being attacked in that alley, I thought that I was going to die, and I knew that sometime Aleck, doing his own research, would find out about my background, and would think that I'd never loved him, that I'd married him as part of a treasure hunt. And then when I was myself again, I knew by Aleck's manner that he *had* found out, just as I'd feared, and . . . oh, it was an awful time. Just awful."

"A time which is over," Holmes suggested kindly.

Winnie broke into a glorious smile. "Oh *yes*, Mr. Holmes. Over now."

"Why did you follow us to Nightsead?" I asked. "In fact, how did you know where we were going?"

Winnie gave me a condescending look of female superiority. "I didn't know where you and Mr. Holmes were going, Doctor Jack, but I certainly knew where Aleck was headed—did you really think that I wouldn't? Oh, he didn't *tell* me, but I knew."

"You understand one reason that I am unmarried, Watson?" Holmes commented drily.

Winnie wrinkled her little nose at him. "I wasn't going to be left out of anything, Mr. Holmes, so I just kept out of the way. At least I thought that I had until you called up to me among those rocks. When did you first spot me?"

"When we were getting on the train here in London," Holmes replied, with a small smile of his own. "And again in Wrinehill when I saw a lad with a horse—with a side-saddle already on his back—waiting behind the station-house. I knew that you had sent a few telegrams of your own, and I was not surprised: you are a determined young lady, Mrs. Raleigh. How is Dan Thatcher?"

Winnie's face softened into a look quite maternal. "Just fine. He's attending a sort of private prep school that a retired minister runs (Aleck calls it a 'swot hole') and will be starting at the University of London next year, in medicine. It's wonderful for Aleck, you know: he's always been so lonely, and now he has a family." She rose to leave. "There's just one more thing: would you both care to attend a private service next month at Hayes Barton?"

"Where Sir Walter Raleigh is buried." Holmes gave a quick nod. "Is the service to be on the twenty-ninth, by any chance?"

"I knew you'd understand. Yes, it is: on the day on which Sir Walter Raleigh was executed. We've found a most considerate clergyman who is arranging everything very quietly so that no one else need ever suspect.

"Did you know," she turned from the door, "that King James released Raleigh from the Tower only on the condition that he find gold in the New World, and that, when the expedition failed, all his friends expected that he would take refuge on the Continent? But Raleigh refused: he had given his word and he kept it. He returned to England, knowing that he faced certain death. When the headsman's axe descended, a great hush fell over the crowd, and then a voice cried out, 'We have not another such head to be cut off!' If there had been nothing else under that Nightsead stone, I would still feel that Aleck and I had a rich legacy." With a final smile, she had gone.

We sat for some moments in silence, for indeed there seemed nothing to say. Then Holmes, softly, and as if speaking into the dusk, began to recite:

> *O cruel Time, which takes in trust*
> *Our youth, our joys and all we have,*
> *And pays us but with age and dust,*
> *Who in the dark and silent grave*
> *When we have wandered all our ways*
> *Shuts up the story of our days.*
> *And from which earth and grave and dust*
> *The Lord shall raise me up I trust.*

"Raleigh wrote that on the night before his execution. Perhaps, Watson, Mrs. Raleigh's tribute is not too high."